THE ONLY GOOD ONE IS A DEAD ONE

A study on African snakes showing how alike in character they are to the devil.

Published by: **OUT OF AFRICA PUBLISHERS**
P.O. Box 34685
KANSAS CITY, MO 64116
U.S.A.

Web:www.kalibu.org
Email:shekmin@aol.com

All scriptures quoted are out of the King James Version of the Bible unless otherwise notated.

Our grateful thanks to Albert for the sketches. May he use his talents for the glory of God.

Printed in the United States of America
ISBN 1-888529-01-6

TABLE OF CONTENTS

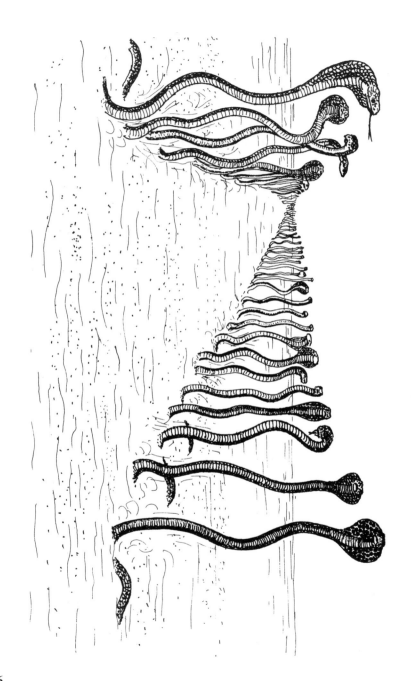

CHAPTER ONE

THE VISION

I am a snake hater, how about you? If not, by the end of this book I hope you will be one too! One night I had a most vivid vision. It was so real that afterwards I was drenched in sweat. That however, turned me into a militant, crusading Christian.

In the vision I was walking across a vast, unending plain. It was not normal or natural and it was absolutely flat. The entire area was covered with thick, fine ash as if a huge volcano had spewed forth but I knew that the plain had been created by the results of an atomic fall-out. There was not a tree, river, hill or building in sight. Cities had been completely destroyed. In fact the whole earth had been annihilated and everything turned to ash. I was alone as I trudged across that vast plain leaving deep footprints in the soft powder. This was a true wilderness: desolate, foreboding, even frightening. I did not know from where I was coming or to where I was going. I was totally alone. How many know that that is the time when God can deal with you? People are afraid to be alone; quiet and separated from family and friends. It's unnatural, yes, but it is spiritual. A soft wind whipped up the ash against my legs. I was tired and somewhat dejected.

Now I'm a true African and like all Africans I have a deep hatred for snakes. The only good snake is a dead one. Africans for the most part are very different from Indians who love dabbling with snakes. God will often use those things of which we are afraid, not only to give us victory over our fears, but to teach other valuable lessons.

Suddenly, as I trudged along, an enormous line of snakes emerged out of the dust. The bodies of those creatures stood up high as they advanced towards me hissing and spitting with flaming eyes. The incredible thing was that their advance was totally disciplined and ordered. I did the most natural thing: I turned and ran. To my utmost horror a similar line of snakes arose. I was trapped on an "avenue" with a "hedge" of snakes demarcating the avenue. The terrifying problem was that the avenue was narrowing as the snakes advanced on me. Frantically I turned to the left side. A line of snakes arose in that direction. I wheeled right and advanced a few paces but in similar fashion, a final army of snakes rose to encompass me on all four sides. The hissing of that multitude of serpents was deafening. They spat and waved to-and-fro on their tails like seaweed on the ocean floor: I was panic-stricken and knew that there was no way out of that horrendous situation.

Instantly, the noise and spitting ceased. The silence in turn was petrifying. Out of the midst of the serpents arose the devil himself laughing with a most hideous laugh that echoed and re-echoed across the plain. He appeared as the most terrifying of the serpents and was enshrouded in a greenish, translucent light.

"You're afraid," he shrieked with glee, "I'm going to kill you today...."

"You can't. I belong to God. God Help!" I shouted. With that, the devil laughed in a most macabre fashion.

"Do you not think I know God?" He questioned. "Why, God created me. I know Him and I'm not afraid of Him," he continued.

"Jesus!" I screamed frantically, but the devil interjected again,

"Oh, I met Him in the wilderness and I'm not afraid of Him. I tempted Him." He laughed as the serpents moved closer and closer. I decided to try the last person of the Trinity.

"Holy Spirit," I called hoping for a mighty deliverance.

"He cannot help you. God has forsaken you," snarled the devil. "I will finish you off."

By this time I was desperate, knowing that if the Lord didn't come through immediately, I was dead. It seemed that there was no power to stop those serpents from devouring me and devour me they would. I cried out to the Lord quietly in my heart to give me the answer. The serpents, had by then, formed a complete circle around me and were advancing upon me for their *coup-de-gras*.

Suddenly, the still small voice of the Lord whispered, "It is the Blood! The power is in the Blood!" Instantly, I felt as if I had grown several feet taller. In a moment the devil and all his serpents seemed rather insignificant. One word from God is enough and He'd just given me the key to victory in that horrendous predicament.

Lifting my hand, I pointed directly at Satan and shouted, **"THE BLOOD! THE BLOOD!! THE BLOOD!!!"** The grotesque form of Satan contorted as he screamed, **"NO, NO, NO!"** I began to advance towards him and commanded repeatedly, "By the Blood of Jesus, by the Blood of Jesus, by the Blood of Jesus, you are defeated by the Blood of Jesus......." By that time, all the serpents had taken up the cry, "No, no, no." It was not a cry of argument but a cry of torment. They did not want to hear the very word "Blood." In a moment every serpent completely disappeared and I was left alone upon that plain. There was such victory! Since that day, I have been a militant campaigner and warrior against satan and his workers. That is not to say my life is taken up with the devil and demons but the devil and all demons were completely defeated at the Cross by the Blood of Jesus.

The Blood cannot be activated in your life unless you are living a separated, holy life and walking in righteousness. Be warned not to take on the devil if your walk is not what it should be. The Sons of Sciva were beaten up by demons for the simple reason that they did not know Paul's Christ. Acts 19:15 *"and the evil spirit answered and said, Jesus I know and Paul I know; but who are ye"*. Many of the native Christians of Africa who are not in right standing with the Lord will not touch demoniacs fearing the devils will come out of the demoniac into them. I have witnessed such things happen. At the same time, I had a man travel all the way from Zambia asking for Bonnke or myself. "Why?" I asked.

"Because I know that if either of you pray for me I will be set free from the demons which possess me and continually torment me," he replied. "The demons told me they hate you both. I know they are afraid of you so you must be the one to help me." I was excited that the demons and the devil know me by name. It really says something!

How many of you realize that in these last days in which we are living, the final battleground is already planet Earth? The war has come down from the heavenlies and is being fought out right here on earth. It is no wonder that we are experiencing an unprecedented explosion of demonic, supernatural, activity. Man is quite happy to co-habit with devils and has gone to great lengths to make demonic creatures not only acceptable, but to be embraced. E.T. is a demon and not the sweet friend of some child. Dinosaurs are demonic and not cute. Our children have been seduced and deceived into accepting the abnormal and demonic as normal. This is in preparation for when demons will not only possess human bodies as they do now but will manifest and masquerade in other forms.

Christians sadly have also been seduced and have lost their fighting power. The Church which Jesus said He is building is a militant, victorious Church. It is against this background that I learned to hate and fight not only the works of the devil but the devil himself and his agents.

Don't be content to co-habit with the devil. Too many Christians are lulled into passiveness. They wake up one day to find their power and strength are gone and with them their joy and peace. Why? Because they have been sleeping with the enemy. Know your enemy: he's not cute. He's out for your life. He may come *appearing* as an angel of light but he's not. That handsome hulk that *you* married because your flesh became all goosey, turned out to be filled with sex devils, drunken devils and every other devil who seeks to draw you away from God and His victory. That sweet little blonde has turned out to be a "she-witch." Do you get the picture friend? Don't keep your devil a secret and don't ever pamper his or her whims because you will quickly plunge into deeper bondage. Expose the hidden works of darkness because they are unfruitful. In fact, Ephesians commands us to have

"no fellowship with the unfruitful works of darkness but rather reprove them. (Eph 5:11).

From Genesis 3:15 *"and I will put enmity between thee and the woman, and between they seed and her seed.."*

until the devil is finally cast into the lake of fire in Revelation there will always be war. Believer, as much as you were born and then born again, so as much are you plunged into a war of which you have no choice. Jesus' death on the cross was not so much to destroy satan but to bring us back into harmony and fellowship with God. The Lord has given His children the privilege to overcome the enemy by the *"Blood of the Lamb and the Word of our testimony."* (Rev 12:11). When we enjoy a dynamic relationship with God through the access we have with boldness into His very presence because of the Blood of Jesus, then and only then do we have authority and power. Then, when we speak the Word as an oracle, it will have force because of our relationship. What Christians need to do in these days is spend time developing their relationship with God and not to focus on the devil and demons. There has been far too much time devoted to demons. I well remember a pastor taking over the church I had formerly pastored. The presence of God was always awesome in the sanctuary. Because of the new pastor's personal insecurities, he always spent much time, "Binding the devil and demons." One day I confronted him:

"Des," I said, "The devil is not here! I only feel the presence of God and have spent a great price in prayer and fasting for the Lord to visit this church. I object to you always binding the devil. You will eventually attract his attention. Forget about him and concentrate on Jesus."

"Well Michael, I always feel like there's bondage...."

"Because it's in your own life. Really Des, if you do continue speaking and shouting at the devil he will become interested," I insisted.

A few months later, I had cause to visit Des and the church I had once pastored. Sure enough, there was absolute bondage and a real presence of the enemy lurking. I thank God that the so-called "deliverance ministry" of the '80's is finally over. Yes, there is a place for deliverance or casting out demons from a person but I believe some of those in the "deliverance ministry" were so locked up into satan that they often caused people to become possessed by too much focus on devils. They then had to cast out those devils.

There are several factors that must be thoroughly remembered in fighting a war:

    1) Learn to recognize the enemy
    2) Know his tactics
    3) Discern his goals

RECOGNIZE THE ENEMY

Sometimes it is hard to recognize the enemy because he loves a disguise. In my book "Recklessly Abandoned," I shared some of my involvement in the Rhodesian terrorist war. A terrorist war is very different from conventional warfare. It is difficult to recognize the enemy because he masquerades in different guises. During the day the terrorist would put on ragged clothes and live and work as ordinary peasant farmers. At night he would change into camouflage, carry an AK 47 rifle and go around killing. The devil and his army are like terrorists. He *appears* as an angel of light but he is not. You might be living with a devil and not even realize it. That is why Jesus says in John 7:24 *"Judge not according to appearance but judge righteous judgment."*

That is why we have been given the gift of discerning of spirits so that we might not be seduced and ensnared by the enemy. I remember when, as a young pastor at age 20, a man arrived at the church one day. He met the Senior Pastor who was full of how wonderful the man, Jeff was. Jeff was so talented he said, and could do this and that and would be such a wonderful blessing to the fellowship. I just simply had to meet Jeff.

I was in my office the next morning when Jeff arrived. The Pastor, twice as old as myself, bounced in and virtually dragged me out to meet Jeff. He was a tall blonde-haired man, all smiles. He put out one of the largest hands I'd ever seen but as my hand made contact, I withdrew it immediately. He smiled and gushed and was just too pleasant. I knew he had a devil. He appeared to be a good family man with a fine wife and two children but he had a devil and I knew it. From our first meeting, he knew that I had discerned him and he went after me to try to befriend me BUT he was full of the enemy.

After the initial meeting the Pastor was furious. "How could you treat Jeff like that?" He questioned.

"Because he's full of the devil," I replied.

"You have no right to judge. You don't even know him."

"No, I discerned him," I declared, "And the devil will use him to break up this church unless you deal with it."

"I can't believe you are behaving like this...."

And so the conversation continued. Notice the typically Charismatic/Pentecostal religious response: "You have no right to judge...." Yes, we do beloved. Judge righteously according to God's standards but judge we certainly must.

Well, four years later, the church split and Jeff moved on to another church within the denomination to do the same thing. I attempted to warn that pastor too, but his response was just the same -- "Michael, you're being too hard and judgmental."

KNOW HIS TACTICS

The tactics of the devil are many and varied. He has a battle plan to get you. He will attack boldly and blatantly as a roaring lion to frighten you. If that method does not work he will approach as a slippery snake with suggestions and innuendoes and sweet talk. Paul says in 2 Cor 2:11 *"Lest satan should get advantage of us: for we are not ignorant of his devices."* The word "devices" in the Greek is "nomea" which means mind set. We are therefore not ignorant of the ideas that he plants in our minds: he planted rebellion in the mind of Eve. Beware of the lies which seduce us to the *"lust of the flesh, the lust of the eyes and the pride of life."* (1Jn 2:16)

DISCERN HIS GOALS

The goal of the serpent is your ultimate destruction. But, praise God, the serpent is overcome by the *"Blood of the Lamb and the Word of our testimony,"* according to Rev 12:11. Now, what is our testimony? Rev. 19:10 declares that, *"The testimony of Jesus is the spirit of prophecy."* What does this mean? Well, it means that when the fire of Jesus burns inside of you to the exclusion of any other "fire or desire" then you step over into another realm. You are not a normal Christian anymore. Your speech is not normal, your songs are not normal, and your prayers are not normal. You will begin to take on an anointing and an authority called the prophetic anointing. To be a snake fighter, you have to have this prophetic anointing that gives power over ALL the works of the enemy. Having the prophetic anointing does NOT make you a prophet. The spirit of prophecy is declaring the anointed Word of God and since Jesus is the anointed One and our lives are totally sold out for Him, we become "Another man." (1Sam 10:6 *And the spirit of the Lord will come upon thee, and thou shalt prophesy with them, and shalt be turned into another man.* That should be the goal of every believer so as to thwart the purposes of the serpent in your life and the lives of friends and family.

CHAPTER TWO

SNAKE BITE

In Africa we have many deadly poisonous snakes. The Boomslang is a thin grass green snake that lives in trees, hence its name boom (tree) and slang (snake). They usually wait in very leafy trees for an unsuspecting prey to pass underneath before dropping on it and biting it.

The venom of a newly born snake is as deadly as that of a fully grown one. Amongst the deadliest are the cobra and a particularly aggressive snake called a mamba. The mamba comes in two kinds: the green and the black. The latter is a very ferocious snake and tends to wait along pathways for some innocent victim.

I remember driving along a bush road when suddenly a very large black mamba began to cross the track in front of me. I accelerated, fully intending to drive over it. That too can be dangerous because they are so agile they can sometimes twist themselves around the shaft on a vehicle or find a place in the engine and when the vehicle comes to a stop they emerge and attack. A woman was once driving along an African road and ran over a mamba. She was going slowly because of the condition of the road. It was a hot, humid day and all of her windows were down. That demonic creature managed to hook into the tailgate of the vehicle which was a station wagon and slide through the back window. The snake actually attacked and bit the woman as she drove along. Fortunately, she was able to reach a mission hospital in time to get help. It can take seventeen minutes from the time of bite until paralysis sets in and death when a black mamba bites.

As I approached this mamba it rose clear up off the ground and seemed to look me straight in the eyes before bending back to strike. I rejoiced that there was a windshield between the creature and myself. We hit the snake at speed and obviously seriously damaged its back as it was twisting round and round in circles on the ground. My faithful workers leapt from the vehicle to kill it. Despite its injuries the mamba mustered all its strength for an attack on one of the workers. My timely intervention saved him from a fatal bite and we stoned the creature to death from a safe distance. We instantly made a fire on the road and burned the snake. This is important in Africa because a snake which is killed leaves a "death trail." The scent of death attracts the mate which will soon appear and attack anyone in the vicinity of its dead partner. It will also often proceed to eat the dead snake. Natives are very superstitious about this and think that the snake resurrects because next morning there is a trail but no snake! When I lived in the jungles of Mocambique one of the RENAMO army camp commanders had much trouble with snakes. He would always find them sleeping in his room or laid across the threshold of his door. He would kill them and sure enough a few days later, another would come. The man became greatly concerned and felt he was going to die. But, what was happening was that the death scent was being left as the snakes were killed. Once we began to burn their bodies and pray, no more snakes appeared.

How like demons these creatures are! When the "death" smell is on a person, that person tends to attract other demons. Keep away from people with demons unless you are there to cast them out. People and ministries who are tainted with death will always spend much time talking about the devil and demons. As I said, this does nothing but gives him a place and attracts his attention. Often people do smell and it's not because they are sick but because they have demons which put out an odor. Sometimes in ministry you meet people with the foulest breath and it's not because they failed to brush their teeth! It is because of some devil that has been made comfortable, co-habitating with them. I hate foul breath: it shows something is wrong: go and see a doctor or get delivered. People are too fond of blaming the water, food or their nasal passages. It is time to quit the excuses and face the facts. Some of the native pastors eat the green stomach tripe and intestines of the cow as it is their favorite delicacy. When it is cooking it smells nauseating but they never have bad breath or gastric problems after having eaten that rotten stuff.

My godfather owned a farm with large chicken run. One afternoon there was a great commotion in the run. Grabbing his shotgun, he rushed out to find a black mamba eating the eggs. As he approached, the deadly creature rose up to strike. My godfather blasted the mamba with a good dose of lead, severing the head from the body. Whilst the body lay on the ground contorting, the head proceeded to advance towards him, snapping as it came. He did the wisest thing and fled. Should that head have bitten him he would certainly have died.

It has been discovered that the venom of the snake is made up of high doses of concentrated protein which the body is unable to absorb. Once that protein enters the blood stream, it will attack different parts of the body depending on the type of snake. Some poisons attack the nervous system, some the respiratory system and others the muscular system. Few people ever survive the bite of a snake like the mamba but some have managed. In medicine today they are now giving a blood transfusion to those who have been bitten. This means taking the blood of somebody who has survived a deadly snake bite and introducing it into the victim. The antibodies which have built up in the blood of a survivor will help the blood of the victim to fight back and overcome the poison.

In many primitive tribes a mother will introduce minute quantities of snake venom into a child's diet from an early age. The child grows up with a natural immunity to most snake venom and if bitten the poison is not fatal as there are strong antidotes already in the blood. When the serpent "bit" Eve, the poison entered into all of mankind through her blood. That is what is meant when we say we are "born in sin." The venom of that old serpent, satan, the devil, has corrupted the blood of every living person. What is needed is an antidote and this, God has provided. We will look into the antidote in detail in the next chapter.

It is quite amazing how antidotes and the different healing properties that God has given through nature work to combat strong poisons. We have in Africa, a snake called the "Spitting Cobra." I was spat upon once by such a creature and fortunately the venom only sprayed my arms and spectacles but it certainly set up an allergic reaction. This cobra goes for the eyes and seldom misses. It spits with great accuracy and can cause almost

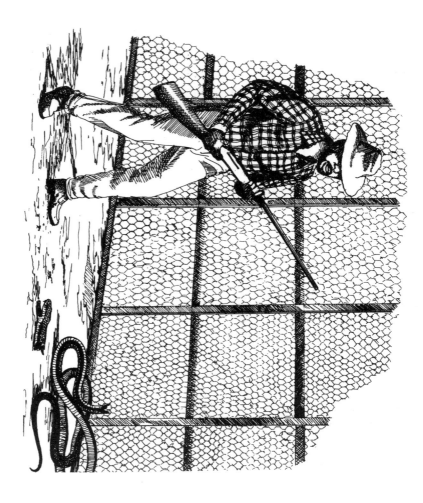

immediate blindness. The searing pain of the poison in the eyes is so severe and excruciating that it causes a person to immediately break into intense vomiting and a drenching sweat. The Bible teaches that the enemy of man, the serpent has blinded the eyes and minds of men that they might not receive the glorious Gospel Jn.12:40 *"he hath blinded their eyes and hardened their heart;"* and 2 Cor 4:4 *"in whom the god of this world hath blinded the minds of them which believe not, least the light of the glorious gospel of Christ, who is the image of God, should shine unto them.'*

Back in the 1950's the rural police in Rhodesia still did most of their patrols on horseback. One of the officers was way out in the bush. He dismounted to investigate some tracks when a cobra spat in his eyes. Very fortunately the policeman was found by a native boy who led him back to the village. Some of the women who were suckling babies used their milk to wash his eyes. They continued the "treatment" for several days at the end of which the policeman was not only able to see but he did not have any lasting eye damage. Milk became the strong antidote for the poison.

I remember being in a remote jungle area with my truck which runs on two 12 volt batteries. A young man approached saying that he had been bitten by a snake. He lifted his trousers to reveal a very nasty bite that was almost turning gangrenous. His whole leg was crusted and scaly and the wound was daily growing bigger. The poison had not been strong enough to kill but it was gradually breaking down his body. It is proven that the strong protein of the venom is both positively and negatively charged. If the charges in the venom can be neutralized, then it will have no power to destroy. I had some thick pieces of copper wire which I connected to the terminals of the battery and I "jumpered" the young man's leg by placing the other ends of the copper wire into the wound. Within days, the leg was completely healed and the wound had closed up.

We have to know how to neutralize the bite of the serpent. It is imperative not only for our very survival but for our progress and victory in the war which every believer is called to fight.

CHAPTER THREE

THE ANTIDOTE

Now the Word of God is absolutely clear that "the serpent was more subtle." The word serpent means "snake," the root word of which means a "whisperer" or "enchanter." It is one who diligently observes to find the weakness and then works upon it to gain entry or access.

It is obvious that the serpent must have moved upright before he was cursed by God. All snakes must stand up to strike and the mamba can stand with only a small portion of its body resting on the ground. It is obvious too, that the serpent could speak for he had a comprehensible conversation with Eve and seduced her. Because of this, God directly cursed in the strongest terms, the serpent. I cannot understand anybody who likes snakes or keeps them as pets. Such a person is sick or possessed. The serpent can never be the friend of man: there is enmity between us and always will be. The devil used the serpent to gain access to Eve. Just as the serpent enchanted Eve, so snakes can also be enchanted in turn. I have watched the snake charmers in India. As they begin to play their flutes and open their baskets, the deadly cobras rise up and begin to dance. Just as long as the music is playing those serpents remain under control. Perhaps it is because the devil was the minister of music in heaven before his fall that the heart of the serpent desires music.

A missionary in India was sharing how, one evening they sat down to dinner. No sooner had they returned thanks for the meal when a large cobra slid over the roof beam above them and dropped on to the table. The hostess told her guests to remain quite still as she slid over to the piano and began to play a soft melody. The snake was instantly mesmerized while one of the guests went and called a native who overcame the creature.

The snake is greatly worshipped in occult and false religions and in India they have entire temples dedicated to snakes which are fed and entertained and then used in religious ceremonies. It is totally demonic.

In the south part of Malawi there is a large python and though I have not seen it, I am told on good authority that the snake is worshipped. The creature lives in a cave and is taken care of by an old witch. The diet of the serpent: young virgins. The serpent is supposed to have knowledge and intuition which can only be demonic. When this snake moves about it has total right of way: when it travels along a path, any person must get out of the track and men must raise their hats to the creature. That's sick but true, and people are terrified of that python. That is exactly how the devil works: he operates through fear by establishing imaginations in the minds of men: that noema of which I spoke in Chapter One.

I have cast out many demons in Third World countries that I call "snake devils." They cause the people to writhe and twist, and to hiss and spit just like a snake. In Chad, West Africa, we have heard tell of women who have visited the witch-doctor to get pregnant and have given birth to snakes. The moment such people are delivered they become normal.

Whilst doing a huge baptismal service once, a woman filled with "snake" devils started going berserk in the water. She twisted and contorted and seemed literally to ooze through our fingers until those demons were commanded to let her alone. There was a great hissing and spitting as the woman was freed.

Anybody who has pet snakes or enjoys playing with them needs deliverance. Snakes are subject to the instincts of the lower nature. A family in London kept a pet python. They were so proud of their snake and always boasted about how obedient the creature was. Well, the family went away for a weekend and returned to find their "pet" was missing. Everybody went to sleep that night, the baby in his crib and next morning when mother went into the bedroom, the baby was gone and the python was asleep in the crib. The snake had a lump half way along its body! Snakes have loyalty to no-one. The devil and demons have no loyalty and no respect for men or each other. They are assigned to be destructive forces and the devil hates man and seeks to destroy him.

Remember, there will always be enmity between men and snakes. God says in His Word, *"And I will put enmity between thee and the woman and between thy seed and her seed: it shall bruise thy head and thou shalt bruise his heel."* (Gen 3:15). In Gen 49:17 the tribe of Dan is likened *to "a serpent by the way, an adder in the path that biteth the horse's heels so that his rider shall fall backwards."*

The devil will never go for those who are strong and victorious: he always works through the lower nature. The serpent was cursed to move on its belly and eat dust. Man was formed of the dust of the earth. Flesh is dust and the serpent always eats dust. The devil will always attack the lower nature of man getting in through the flesh: the lust of the eyes, the lust of the flesh and the pride of life.

In the Word, "Wood" always speaks of humanity. In Acts, when Paul the Apostle reached the island of Melita after the storm and shipwreck, he gathered a bundle of sticks. As he was applying the sticks to the fire, *"There came a viper out of the heat, and fastened on his hand."* Acts 28:3. When men are placed in the fire of God's dealings the serpent nature will always emerge and get exposed under the heat and pressure. That serpent of flesh will attack, fight, devour and kill. For men to change and for the serpent to be burned utterly, humanity must endure the fire of God's dealings. It is precisely for this reason that the church is so fleshly and has no power: it is a carnal church. Evident proof is abundant: the lack of love, the vicious talk and behavior, the amount of suing, the selfishness and greed are all indicative of flesh. There is little display of the fruit of the Spirit in the modern church and the main reason for our weakness and failure to be a pure, spotless, and Holy separated church is because we have taken the "Cross" or death messages out of the Gospel. **WHAT WE ARE NOT READY TO DIE FOR WE CERTAINLY ARE NOT READY TO LIVE FOR**.

The tribe of Dan is likened to a serpent by the way that *"biteth the horse heels."* We know perfectly well that when a horse encounters a snake it will bolt, causing the rider to fall backwards into the hand of the enemy. When the serpent bites the heel it means that he attacks the weak elements of the flesh. Let me explain with an illustration.

Every major army that has ever invaded Russia has made the same tactical error. Any commander must know that their armies should never get caught in a Russian winter. The end of Napoleon was Russia and the beginning of the end of Hitler was Russia. The Russian army has always enticed invaders into their country and ensured that they were trapped by the severe Russian winter. Since the Russians know their conditions and are adequately prepared, it would be foolish for them to engage the strength of their enemies. Instead, what the Russians have always done has been to nip at the heel of the invading army. As the weaker soldiers grew tired and fell behind slowing down the entire invasion force, they would be killed off by bands of Russian Cossacks who would continually "bite" the heel of the invader. In this way, the invaders would be devoured from the weak heel towards the strong head. The devil works in the same fashion. He gets in at the point of weakness and slowly but systematically devours or corrupts through that weak heel. Before long, he has managed to totally overwhelm a Christian in the same way that the Russians always overwhelmed their invaders. When the devil wants to come against a strong local Body he does not attack the strong leadership of that Body but he will work through the weaker brethren. Sometimes this may mean legalism like imposing doctrines of dress and food. In the early church the believers were bewitched into going back to the laws of Judaism and the perverted "gospel" of Gnosticism. At other times the devil might engage weaker vessels in gossip, backbiting and criticism of the fellowship and its leaders. Any weakness in dealing with such situations will allow the enemy to devour the "army of the Lord" by biting the heel and then systematically working its way through the body.

When the serpent "bit" Eve the poison of that bite entered the entire bloodstream of mankind. Paul says in Rom 5:12, *"Wherefore, as by one man sin entered into the world, and death by sin; and so death passed upon all men, for that all have sinned."* He continues in 1Cor 15:45, *"The first Adam was made a living soul, the last Adam was made a quickening spirit."* Thus, *"In Adam all die, even so in Christ shall all be made alive."* 1Cor 15:22. Christ's Blood is the perfect antidote for the serpent bite. He became the key of death and hell, having conquered both at the

Cross. His Blood gives all who receive it the power to fight back against the poison of the enemy. Without it, no man can have any power to overcome devils.

The Blood of Jesus was shed five times:-

1) In the Garden of Gethsemane Jesus sweat drops of blood to break the curse of the stubborn will of man. He said, *"Let this cup pass from me, nevertheless, not as I will, but as Thou wilt."* Matt. 26:39. He showed us a way, a perfect way to submit our wills to the will of Almighty God.

2) They scourged Jesus. The Bible declares that, *"With His stripes we are/were healed."* Is.53:5 and 1Pet. 2:24. The Blood of Jesus has washed away every sickness and disease that came through the poisonous bite of that old serpent, the devil. If you are sick and diseased, receive your healing as you read this. His Blood was shed to purify you from all sickness and disease. Then, having received healing, continue to live under the glory and you will experience Divine Health.

3) Matt 27:29 declares, *"And when they had plaited a crown of thorns they put it upon his head..."* Part of the curse in Genesis was that while the serpent would eat dust (or flesh), man would sweat to bring forth the produce of the earth which in itself would bring forth *"thorns and thistles....."* Gen 3:18. It never ceases to amaze me in Africa how quickly the thorn bushes grow. Dig them out and by the next season when it comes time to plant again, the thorns and thistles have already sprung up. It is a very uncomfortable job clearing away those thorns and weeds under the hot African sun so as to prepare the lands again for another planting. We have been redeemed from the curse of the law by the Precious Blood of Jesus who took upon His brow that curse in the form of a crown of thorns.

4) The hands and feet were nailed to the cross. Only those with pure hearts and holy hands can approach the Lord. The hands speak of ministry and the feet of our walk, both of which are to be washed by the Blood. The priesthood was required to wash hands and feet in the waters of the laver of the Old Testament Tabernacle and Temple. God expressly commands in Exodus 30:19, *"For Aaron and his sons shall wash their hands and feet, that they die*

not...." The corrupt dealings of sinful man and his corrupt worldly walk have an antidote: the Blood of Jesus.

5) John alone records in Chapter 19:34 that, *"One of the soldiers with a spear pierced His side and forthwith came there out blood and water."* In the old days, people believed that the gods had a strange mixture of blood and a fluid of light. This was called "ichor." When the side of Jesus was pierced and the mixture of blood and water flowed forth, the centurion understood it to be "ichor." Remember the blood of Jesus was never contaminated by sin, sickness or disease which is why His Body never saw corruption in the tomb. This sign caused the centurion to declare Jesus to be the Son of God.

When God opened the side of Adam and took out a "rib" what He really did was to take out a bride. Similarly, when the "door" or side of Jesus was opened it was to birth the Bride of the church through the Blood and water.

By His Blood we are saved, delivered, healed. The Blood of Jesus was finally spilt to cover the curse of sin once and for all. The antidote was complete. The smallest application of the Blood is sufficient to neutralize the curse, the bite, the sting, of the serpent. Heb 9:22 declares, *"Without shedding of Blood is no remission [of sin]."* 1Jn 1:9 continues to offer great hope that, *"If we confess our sins He is faithful and just to forgive us our sins and to cleanse us from all unrighteousness."* In Shakespeare's play "Macbeth", Lady Macbeth declares, "Here's the smell of the blood still. All the perfumes of Arabia will not sweeten this little hand." And Macbeth asks, "Will all great Neptune's ocean wash this blood clean from my hand?" All they needed was one drop of the Blood of Jesus.

In Numbers 21:6-9 Moses describes how the children of Israel murmured in the wilderness against God and against him. The Lord sent fiery serpents.

"And the Lord sent fiery serpents among the people, and they bit the people; and much people of Israel died. Therefore the people came to Moses and said, We have sinned, for we have spoken against the Lord, and against thee; pray unto the Lord, that he take away the serpents from us. And Moses prayed for the people. And the Lord said unto Moses, Make thee a fiery serpent and set it

upon a pole: and it shall come to pass that everyone that is bitten, when he looketh upon it shall live. And Moses made a serpent of brass and put it upon a pole, and it came to pass, that if a serpent had bitten any man, when he beheld the serpent of brass, he lived." These fiery serpents are desert adders. They have a very vicious bite which causes the body to break into crusty sores much like leprosy. The condition grows worse and worse through stages of complete paralysis and eventually death.

Now, the bite of the serpent has filled all of us with the poison of sin. I have seen the bite of the desert adder. The legs of the victim swelled to an enormous size and became crusty until they began to break into suppurating sores. The victim finally died. The backbiters and murmurers were bitten and filled with the poison of the adder just as backbiters and murmurers are filled with the poison of the serpent.

God commanded Moses to make of brass the image of the desert viper which had caused such havoc in the ranks of Israel. Brass speaks of judgment and the prince of this world was to be judged at Calvary. Jesus said even as *"Moses lifted up the serpent in the wilderness, even so must the Son of man be lifted up...."* Jn 3:14.

The only requirement for those Israelites bitten by the serpents was that they should LOOK upon the brazen image. This was a type of Jesus on the cross. If they looked, only looked, not only would they be healed from the diseases of their bites but they would be spared from death. You see, God's judgment came upon the brazen serpent but Israel had to look and believe by faith:

> "Look and live my brother live
> Look to Jesus now and live
> 'Tis recorded in His Word Hallelujah
> That you only have to look and live."

Now, the most incredible thing was that as the bitten of the children of Israel were gathered and laid around that serpent, many refused to look at it because they did not believe that by merely looking at a brazen serpent they would be freed. Such unbelief reigned in many hearts despite the fact that they witnessed their friends and neighbors healed and live!

You say that's incredible. No, the same happens today. Though many friends and family see you look to Christ and get healed and delivered from death, yet still they will not believe.

The serpent was judged and condemned at the Cross and the Holy Spirit gives emphasis of this in Jn 16:11 when Jesus says of the Holy Spirit, *"He will reprove the world of sin and of righteousness, and of judgment......Of judgment, because the prince of this world is judged."*

CHAPTER FOUR

CRUSH THE HEAD

In Hong Kong they have the "Avenue of Snakes." Hundreds of Chinese keep deadly snakes in cages which they offer for sale. An amazing ritual that takes place is a counterfeit and mockery of the Communion of the Lord.

The buyer chooses his snake which is then taken from the cage. Carefully, the seller "milks" the snake, catching its poison in a special goblet. Having extracted the poison from its fangs, the snake is then hanged on a hook and sliced open exposing the liver and heart which are extracted and crushed. Together with these organs, a drop of the venom, some blood from the snake and a little wine, a potion is concocted which the buyer then drinks. This potion, it is believed, acts as an aphrodisiac to give sexual potency and increased fertility. Having drunk of the potion, the buyer crushes the head of the snake and is free to take the body home to eat. Such a ritual is of course satanic and no different from the pagan rituals that incorporate the rites of drinking blood whether human or animal. The procedure outlined certainly opens those who practice it to the strongest demon powers.

We have a little wild animal in Africa called a mongoose. I suppose it is about the size of a large squirrel but without the bushy tail. The mongoose is the only animal that can outmaneuver a snake. It is so fast and agile that it can quickly attack and paralyze a snake by attaching itself to the back of the head. This prevents the snake from striking. Once the mongoose has buried its teeth deep into the snake and killed it, it proceeds to eat the head.

When I visited India I delighted to watch a mongoose kill a cobra. Indian boys run around with boxes of cobras and a mongoose in a bag. You can buy a snake which is then removed from the box. They release the mongoose from its sack and immediately the fight is on. The mongoose always wins! It's great fun! I always enjoyed seeing any serpent crushed. It is instinctive because the Bible declares that we will tread upon serpents and scorpions.

One day, in Africa, I stepped out on to the verandah (porch) of the house. A huge green mamba was lying across the porch sunning itself. I was furious at this intruder and determined it must die. Grabbing a long-handled broom from the kitchen I slammed it down on the creature with all my might. The broom met with the victim's back inflicting injury. It managed to slither under an elevated drum whereupon the broom handle was rammed into the space inflicting further injury. Moving from there the snake slipped under a raised trash can lid. I slammed the lid to the ground, trapping the creature. Weighing down the lid with the nearest rock I prevented it from escaping after which I collected a large pail of boiling water and poured the entire pail both over and under the lid. That snake was scalded so much that when the lid was removed all it could do was writhe in circles. It was then an easy matter to pulverize the entire head and burn the remains.

Genesis declares that, *"I will put enmity between thee and the woman,"* whose seed would bruise the enemy's head. Now while in the natural there is enmity between men and serpents, there should be the same kind of enmity with the devil, the enemy of our souls. It is time for the Body of Christ to rise up against the enemy. Christians have been too happy co-habitating with the devil. Most believers have been desensitized and are content. It is time that the Church became indignant and angry at all the perversions of satan and his works. Only when a holy anger begins to coat the inner being of every believer will we be able to take authority over the works of the enemy and over the enemy himself. Rhetoric alone will not work: quoting scriptures alone will not work: the devil knows the Scriptures better than most Christians.

In its natural state, the cobra will often enter the tunnels of field mice and find their nests. At first, the mice are fearful but they soon find that the cobra does no harm to them and so they become comfortable "nest partners." The mice think that they can run over the cobra, sleep with it and even play with it. (Sound familiar)? But, a snake is a snake! In the same fashion many Christians have bedded down with the enemy. He comes in dozens of subtle forms and we find that we soon lose the fire and cutting edge of our lives.

When a mouse leaves the nest the cobra will follow it down the tunnel. It is at ease because the snake has become its "friend." It does not realize that upon its return that same snake will have positioned itself for the attack. The mouse is swallowed and when the meal is finished the snake returns to the nest and once again beds down with the remaining mice. They continue to be oblivious to the methods of the snake.

How like the cobra the devil and his workers are. They subtly gain access into a person's life and when that person is least suspecting, they strike and devour.

On the Cross Jesus utterly crushed the head of the serpent. Although He did that in actuality, it is necessary for us to appropriate that reality to make the power effective in our lives. It is an amazing thing that the serpent bites the heel but believers are commanded to crush the head. If a person bitten by a serpent refuses to apply the antidote, he will die. No man, neither Jew nor Roman, no nation and no devil took the life of Jesus. The Lord said, *"No man taketh my life from me, but I lay it down of myself. I have power to lay it down and I have power to take it again."* Jn 10:18.

If the devil had known that the crucifixion of Jesus meant that his head would be crushed, he and the princes of this world, *"Would not have crucified the Lord of Glory."* 1Cor 2:8. When Jesus pronounced on the Cross, *"It is finished,"* Jn 19:30, He was uttering a well-known Latin military term, "Tetilesti." This Latin word for "finished" means complete annihilation of the enemy. In the old days when the Romans went to war they would often engage the enemy in a famous "Ox-horn" formation. The two horns would almost totally surround the enemy while units comprising the "head" would move in to engage the enemy. The Romans would always keep back some crack battalions in reserve, forming a "neck." The Roman generals who were directing their forces occupied elevated ground from which they could observe the entire battlefield. At an appropriate moment, when the enemy was beginning to tire, the general would raise a special flag. The flag symbolized the word "Tetilsti." At the moment that flag was raised, the Roman troops would immediately fall back in mock defeat. The enemy thought they had won and came pouring in on the Romans but as they did, the fresh battalions would swamp in and overwhelm them. The tactic never failed to produce a complete victory.

When satan thought that he had "bruised" Christ's humanity and defeated Him, Christ came storming back and spoiled *"principalities and powers making a show of them openly and triumphing over them in it,"* Col 2:15 and he did it at the Cross and not in hell. This is another Roman military expression. When the Roman legions had won the victory in battle one of their assignments was to capture alive the defeated generals, princes or king. These captives were reserved for the victory ceremony which was always held in Rome. The victorious Roman general would lead his army through the streets of Rome, riding upon a ceremonial chariot to which were chained the defeated generals and king. Often the prisoners would be stripped naked to heighten the humiliation of defeat. The Roman crowds would cheer their victors and mock the defeated. The prisoners would be dragged behind the chariot to the throne of the emperor who would award the victor's baton and laurel wreath and proclaim judgment upon the vanquished.

Jesus made an open show of the devil and all his hordes. His triumph was the victory parade before all principalities and powers for all time. His reward is that He sat down at the right hand of God, (Heb 10:12), crowned as King of kings. The devil was tied to *His* chariot and the ultimate judgment pronounced on him. That old serpent is condemned to the lake of fire forever.

All of what Christ achieved is only potential for us unless we walk in victory. The devil will walk all over you; will rob you, lie to you and destroy your life unless you start to become angry. I remember many years ago seeing one of the series, "Incredible Hulk." When the man was pushed into a corner or provoked until he could no longer stand it, he "**HULKED**." That is exactly what God's people need to do: to **HULK** it with the devil and the world. When you have had enough of being walked upon, of whimping out, of being a grasshopper then you can **HULK** it and start roaring like a lion. Then, and only then will the **POTENTIAL** of all that Christ achieved become **REALITY** in your personal life.

The same applies to the Body of Christ, national and international. A friend of mine had a remarkable vision in which he saw individual Christians crushing the heads of many serpents. It seemed however, that just as soon as they crushed one devil many more sprang to the fight. Those devils were easily able to maneuver amongst Christians and often avoid defeat. There were too few Christians fighting the battle. Then an incredible miracle began to take place as the Spirit of God moved upon multitudes of weak and defeated Christians. As the Christians began to mold together into one body the multitudes of individual feet which were trying to crush the heads of the serpents began to fuse together into two giant feet which covered the whole earth. There was no place for any serpent to wriggle through and every one was crushed under the giant feet of one Body.

Until all believers in the West become disgusted and indignant at the works of the serpent: the lawlessness, abortion, homosexuality, drug addiction, violence and everything else that is an abomination before God, there will be no crushing of the serpent's head. What is it going to take for the giant to awake, rise up and appropriate that which Christ already completed at the Cross? When all believers surrender their personal wills and ambitions; when denominations cease being suspicious of one another; when true love and mutual respect begin to flow and create a Holy Spirit unity, not a man-induced one; when each member of the Body knows his or her place and is secure in Christ and their calling, only then will there be such an outrage that the voice of the world will be silenced. The church must cease to view itself as grasshoppers and become the **"HULK"** and with one huge foot crush the entire head of the serpent. Mouse, get out of the nest and leave it to the cobra. When you least expect it he will devour you.

CHAPTER FIVE

HE'S DEFEATED

Jesus said that we must be, *"Wise as serpents and harmless as doves."* Matt 10:16. Snakes are extremely sensitive and cunning. Unfortunately, they are not harmless as doves. In certain parts of Africa where the python skin is much prized, a native will wrap his leg in lengths of cloth which have been smeared with animal saliva. The saliva attracts the python while the cloth protects the leg from gastric juices. The native will actually put his leg into a hole which he knows is inhabited by a python. Soon, the creature will begin to swallow the leg and when it has swallowed almost to the knee, friends will drag him from the hole bringing the snake with him. They kill the snake and free the native.

My parents who still live in Africa, kept rabbits and often in the early morning Dad would go out to find that a small python had slipped through the wire mesh over night and seized a young rabbit. The only problem was that, having swallowed the animal, the python would become stuck trying to get back out. The creature would remain stuck until morning when Dad would decapitate it. Many years ago he came across a large python that had swallowed an antelope. In swallowing it the horns had pierced through the body of the serpent. It takes many days for a python to digest an animal of that size and during such times the snake is very vulnerable as it cannot move.

Snakes often live in colonies and can be extremely troublesome. It is difficult either to catch them or defeat them because they are very sensitive creatures. One way the natives have found to overcome a colony of snakes is to embed new razor blades in blocks of wood and bury them in the sand around the entrance to the nest. Only the very tip edge of the blade protrudes above the ground. Because the blade is so sharp and the snake slithers

quickly over it, the creature is sliced open before realizing its predicament. Such a method never ceases to produce results.

Of course, there is an easier way to get rid of serpents and it is to command them to go by using the authority and power of the name of Jesus. Again, we have to know and be secure in who we are and what we have in Christ. The point was strongly brought home to me when I went out preaching in the bush some years ago. The area is very hostile with temperatures reaching 120 and the humidity high in the 90's. The only shade in a vast area was one large mango tree. On our arrival, there were several natives standing around and beating the tree with long bamboo poles. It was not the right season for fruit and immediately I knew - a snake! As we alighted from the vehicle we were informed by the pastor that it would be impossible to camp under the tree as there were three deadly snakes in it which they had been trying to chase out for a couple of days. The creatures refused to go.

Instantly, the anger began to rise up within me. I hate snakes, remember. I marched over to that tree. Those snakes were not going to deprive me of the only shade. Pointing my finger at the tree I sternly rebuked, "In the name of Jesus Christ, I command you foul serpents to depart immediately." Instantly, there was a commotion in the thick leaves and one by one in a matter of seconds, the snakes not only fell from the tree with a loud thwack but seemed to flee as if in terror. What a testimony it was to the natives. We never saw those serpents again.

If the natural serpents are sensitive to the Word of God spoken with authority in the prophetic voice how much more must the devil and his demons submit to that same authority?

Many years ago as a very young school teacher, I had a dramatic encounter with the devil himself. It was the school holidays and I was alone in a very large hostel. I had gone down to the staff common room to do some work. It was summer and a still, hot evening. So, leaving the door wide open in the hope of a slight breeze, I embarked on my work. Suddenly an incredible whirlwind whistled around the building and the door slammed with such force that the whole building shook. The hair all over my body was electrified. There was no appearance, only a sinister mocking and laughing. I left the room and walked upstairs. I must confess that I

was momentarily more than a little afraid. The devil was walking behind me. I could hear him but more than that I could sense the incredible evil. At the top of the stairs I realized that it was ridiculous to be fearful and I became indignant and angry partly at my own foolishness and because I did not want this unwelcome visitor which had disrupted my evening. I guess I "hulked," and turning I pointed my finger and with authority commanded, "In the name of Jesus and by His Blood, be gone!" With a shriek and a rattle of the louvers, the enemy fled.

Eight years later, the serpent came again. I was driving in Pennsylvania and visiting some of the places of the great awakenings. I saw a sign advertising the "Tabernacle of Moses." Thinking that someone had built a replica of the Tabernacle I stopped only to find that it was the birthplace of Joseph Smith, founder of the Mormons. As I stood in amazement reading the plaque, the devil arrived in the form of a good-looking businessman, but what evil eyes. There was that same evil presence, so strong that it was almost tangible. With a ghoulish whisper he said three things:

"Today I will kill you!" My instant and indignant reply was, "I belong to Jesus. I'm not yours and you can't kill me."

"Well," he drawled, "If I cannot kill you then I will destroy your reputation."

"I don't have a reputation and I'm not seeking one so you cannot get me on that," I laughed.

"Then I'll destroy your ministry."

"That's not mine either," I countered, "so you're defeated."

With that I left and climbed into my van. I took off down the road and was barely into third gear when the steering was literally snatched from my hand with a vice-like grip. The van careened off the road hitting a mail box. As we started to run along the edge of a steep embankment I knew instantly what had happened. I roared, "JESUS, help!" as I let go the steering. This battle was not mine. The steering was released and the van bounced to an immediate halt in the ditch. I was so furious with that serpent that all I could say was, "Try harder next time and attempt to be original. You've attempted that before. Aren't you tired of road accidents?"

Perhaps you have wondered why certain intersections or places always have accidents? Because of demons that assign themselves to those spots and cause havoc. It's time to crush the serpent in those places and set people free.

A friend of ours lived a block away from a busy intersection in Tulsa, Oklahoma. There were accidents on a regular basis at that intersection, a number of them fatal. One day we decided to redeem that intersection, commanding the spirits to depart and taking authority over the territory. From that moment the accidents there came to a stop. There is no reason why we have to accept the status quo when we have power to change it.

How long will American Christians sit back and watch hurricane after hurricane, flood after flood, fire after fire and one natural disaster after another devastate billions upon billions of property? What is happening is not purely natural. When will the Christian television moguls get down to using what God has given them to mobilize the Body of Christ? We have the power over the elements to deflect hurricanes and tornadoes by our prayers.

2 Chron 14:7 is very clear. *"If MY people which are called by MY name .....I will hear from heaven and HEAL their land."*

Until we appropriate all the potential which Christ won at the cross, we shall never be able to crush the serpent's head and be what God wants us to be. Too many Christians spend too much time focusing on their personal inner turmoil. Look to the Cross and get free.

CHAPTER SIX

PUT DOWN THE FLESH

The saddest thing I have witnessed in Africa is that the witches and warlocks know their god better than most Christians know theirs. God must be the prime motivator in our lives. Let me be frank in saying that, even though I am a devil hater and fighter, I do believe that the devil gets an awfully large amount of blame for things for which he is not responsible.

Remember, the devil is neither omnipotent nor omniscient nor omnipresent. He himself can only be at one place at one time, so he is limited. But he has a myriad of demons who work on his behalf. Now, the devil can put thoughts into our minds but he cannot read our thoughts and intents: that realm is reserved only for the Holy Spirit. Many Christians erroneously believe that the devil cannot understand tongues or our "spiritual" or "heavenly" language as people call it. Paul says, *"Though I speak with the tongues of men and of angels...."* 1Cor 13:1. The serpent, the devil, was once the archangel Lucifer so he understands the tongues of angels. When Paul says, *"For I pray in an unknown tongue, my spirit prayeth but my understanding is unfruitful."* 1Cor 14:14, he is meaning by "unknown tongue" one that is not understood by the speaker. Such a tongue may be an earthly language or an angelic language. Either way, the devil understands. Thus the power of tongues is not that the devil doesn't understand because he does, but that we don't! This is because an unknown (that not understood) tongue by-passes our understanding. The serpent then is neither omnipresent nor omniscient nor all-knowing and neither is he all powerful. As long as we are obedient to God, we can resist him and he must flee. (Ja 4:7).

There are three persons who can directly influence our lives: God, satan and ourselves or humans in general. A man might cram eight people into a six-seater airplane and wonder why the plane crashes. Christians enter into a great debate: Did the devil kill them? Why didn't God protect them? Did God take them home? Why, when he was doing a work for God? None of these answers is correct. The plane crashed because the man was plainly stupid. He attempted to defy the laws of gravity, the laws of nature, and he paid the supreme price. It was the man's fault for overloading the plane. The law of gravity was in operation and the plane crashed.. Leave God out, leave satan out. God has endowed men with plain rational sense and He expects us to use it. Of course, when God directs, or circumstances really demand, supernatural laws supercede natural such as divine transportations and miracles. In fact all the gifts of the Spirit are supernatural operations which supercede or over-ride the natural.

Now, there are definite times when the devil and his demon powers can, and will come against us. Instantly, we should discern the enemy. The Lord clearly declared, *"My sheep hear My voice."* Jn 10:27. And, *"I know My sheep and am known of mine,"* Jn 10:14 so that any other voice is that of the devil, man or self. One time when I was returning from a glorious meeting and right in the midst of praising God, a sudden thought pierced my mind like an arrow: it was demonic: "Curse God!" I instantly rebuked that spirit and continued praising God.

Of course, men are open to demonic attack if there are areas of lust in their lives: that is a heel and the enemy will bite that heel. Close the doors and get free. Many people blame the devil for classic cases of "self." If the doors of your life are open to the devil through lust and sloppy living, then don't blame anyone if you're possessed or oppressed. If you're reading smutty magazines and watching X Rated movies it is no wonder you're attacked with sexual problems and could be possessed.

While doing crusades in India a woman was brought to me for prayer. She was carried by two men. She had been a temple entertainer! Know what I mean? Well, the woman had become possessed with what I call "animal demons." She had an elephant-type face without the trunk. She was gnarled and twisted like a serpent. As we prayed the demons began to come out of her. She hissed and writhed like a snake, her tongue flicking. She spat great green gobs of slime. Then she began to trumpet like an elephant as the "elephant demon" was cast out. She clawed and growled like a tiger as those demons were commanded to leave her body. She bellowed as a bull and grunted and snorted like a pig. As each set of devils left her body, she began to unravel. Oh, her breath was like the worst sewer I have ever smelled! Finally, the woman was totally freed of every devil and stood completely released in mind, body and spirit. Her facial features had changed and she could walk as a normal human being.

In contrast, I was preaching in Kentucky. The meeting had just closed when a woman shrieked and leapt from her chair and collapsed on the floor. She started slithering and spitting. In usual Christian fashion everybody pounced on the woman and began yelling at the demons. This display had continued for sometime with no visible change when the pastor asked me to intervene. I walked over to the writhing woman while telling the congregation to sit down and leave her alone. I did not get so far as to lay my hands on her. I knew this was an incredible display of flesh.

Walking back to the pulpit, I declared, "This is not the kind of disgusting display we need to see in church." "Lady," I addressed her, "You need to quit drawing attention to yourself and seeking man's sympathy. Control your flesh and deliver yourself. This display is not a manifestation and you're not possessed, it's your flesh!"

Suddenly the woman went rigid and dug her fingers into the carpet with humiliation and rage. Found out! The next day she spoke with me and said that I had been the first person to ever speak truthfully to her. At that moment she had hated it but the truth had set her free and she wanted to thank me.

That's flesh and most Christians have it and lots of it and I'm not talking of the calorie kind. All too often, people stand in prayer lines for "deliverance" when they have no devils. What they need is a big dose of self discipline and control to bring some order into their lives. That does not come by some anointed preacher laying hands on you: it comes by hard work. Put the flesh down. Every time your hormones run riot, or your over-inflated body cries for more calories of junk food or you desire to behave like a spoiled screaming brat who cannot have his/her way (this is how the heathen behave and they get demons) submit the flesh to the Cross and live for Jesus

In Galatians 4, Paul speaks of the works of the flesh. They are NOT demons. There is no such thing as a demon of gluttony: it is a lust of the flesh and was learned by habit. What Paul teaches is that Christians enslaved to BAD habits need to re-habitize their lives. Paul clearly teaches, "Put off" the old man and "Put on" the new. In other words, break the cycle of the old habits which led you to sin and establish a new Godly habit pattern. Many people under emotional stress will rush to the refrigerator and eat. Such is a bad habit pattern. There's no demon of gluttony. Putting off such a habit one could establish a new habit pattern of praying until the peace and joy of the Lord descends and relieves one from the emotional crisis which will eventually pass anyway.

It is no wonder that Cain was a murderer. His mother had a "relationship" with the serpent and became demonized. The Bible says that *"He [satan] was a murderer from the beginning,"* Jn 8:44 and that there is no truth in him because he is the father of lies. Eve believed the lie, was deceived and the "man-child" that she claimed *she* had gotten was a murderer after the likeness of his spiritual father.

Whilst preaching in a large Pentecostal church in Portugal I shared of some demonic deliverances from Africa. A woman rushed up with her young daughter. The girl was full of demons. In today's world of psychiatry and sociology she would be called hyper-active or psychoneurotic and that is exactly what the pastor had labeled her as he demanded that I take no action and was not to interfere with his church member. Whispering to the interpreter, I told her to inform the lady to call the house where I was residing. The woman was distraught and she prevailed upon me to assist her during our telephone conversation.

The next day I went down to her home. They were a wealthy family with a beautiful Mediterranean-type villa. The woman told me how they had spent a fortune in Europe taking their child to every pediatrician and expert but to no avail.

"Only Dr. Jesus can solve this problem," I declared. "The problem itself is not so serious but the root is and we must get to the root."

By this stage the young girl was acting like a terrified caged animal. Her eyes flamed. She rushed around the room and then fell, exhausted, into her mother's arms. She lay there for a moment before leaping up again and rushing around once more. Panic was then in her eyes and a whimper came from her lips. She cowered from me as I walked over to her and she began to cry in a pathetic infant way although she was almost twelve. My initial prayer brought little response and I quickly discerned that the girl was possessed because her very "proper" mother was full of demons. I separated the mother and child. While my friend held the girl, I dealt with the mother who began to scream and scream as she was delivered from demon after demon. As the mother became freed the girl was released. By the time the woman was completely delivered, her daughter was also set free and her very appearance and behavior calmed down. The screaming mother and daughter had attracted neighbors who obviously thought I was committing murder.

After the ordeal the mother was so overwhelmed with the victory that she called her friends and neighbors to "come in and see." By the following day over eighty people crowded into the house to hear the Gospel because a daughter had been set free resulting in most of the people receiving Jesus as Savior.

In the next chapter I will relate more real encounters with demoniacs. Suffice to say then, that people need to overcome their fleshly desires and to obey the laws which God has laid down for the governing of society. When we break laws of God or society it is neither the devil nor God when we have to pay the price but it's our own fault. There are real cases of satan's interference directly in a person's life and other cases when God will move but more often we fall under God's universal law of sowing and reaping. If we sow to the flesh we reap confusion, bondage and misery. If we sow to rebellion, we reap rebellion. If we bind others by our attitude and behavior, our relationship with both them and God will be bound, and so on.....

Finally, there is God's direct intervention in our lives. Jer 33:3 declares, *"Call unto Me and I will answer thee and shew thee great and mighty things, which thou knowest not."* Now God always answers prayer but not always when or how we want Him to answer. It is much like the traffic lights at and intersection. There is, "No," "Yes," or "Wait!" Most Christians only want to hear a "Yes" from God and might tolerate a "Wait" answer but when it comes to "No" they do one of three things. Attribute a "No" from God as being of the devil because it does not line up with their whim, seek out other Christians who will agree with them or just ignore God completely and refuse to obey. When Christians cannot accept a "No" answer from God they are on the dangerous ground of entering into "Balaam's Business." Soon, God will allow you to do what you desire even although His will is clear, but you will pay the supreme price as did Balaam.

While preaching in Minneapolis one night a woman came for a word. Well, she received a word but I could tell that she was very unhappy and disgruntled with what she had received. The following evening she came again for another. I am not in the habit of prophesying willy-nilly and was about to pass her by when the Lord impressed upon me to speak over her. The only problem was *that* word was totally opposite from the word she had received the night before. Initially the woman was excited but at the end of the meeting she came to me "very confused." I myself, was questioning the Lord as to what He had done. All He answered was "Balaam's Business."

It is very unfortunate that so many Christians attribute God's interventions in their programs to the devil. In Matt 5:25 Jesus commands us to, *"Agree with thine adversary quickly, whilst thou art in the way with him; lest at any time the adversary deliver thee to the judge, and the judge deliver thee to the officer and thou be cast into prison..."* Most people immediately think of the adversary as the devil and he *is* except in this particular verse. It would be impossible for Jesus to tell us to agree with the devil or his workers. So then, what does Jesus mean? Who is the adversary with whom we must agree? In this particular verse the adversary undoubtedly is the Lord Himself who is showing us a red light which we are either not willing to obey or of which we are truly ignorant. Balaam's adversary was, "The angel of the Lord," who had been sent to stop Balaam in his foolish endeavors. Balaam's problem was that his heart was lusting after the riches which Balak had offered him to curse Israel. God at that stage was

trying to prevent Balaam from doing foolishly and even permitted Balaam to be rebuked by the mouth of an ass. Eventually God will give us over to our lusts but send leanness and confusion into our lives. Many times when Christians are speeding towards a danger zone or disaster, either through stubbornness and rebellion or through sheer ignorance, God will resist their path and attempt to prevent a disaster. At that point, God becomes the adversary because He opposes the will of man. Until such time as there is yielded ness to the will God, a person who is willful will be a slave in chains and remain so until there is agreement with the adversary. This agreement is the "payment" of which Jesus speaks and only when payment and restitution have been made, can the person be released from prison. I remember when I ended up as a prisoner with the rebel movement in Mocambique. During the first couple of days I wrestled with the issue, and the prison I was in was more than just a physical cage. There was a struggle with mental and physical anguish as well as with the Lord. Why had such a situation arisen when I was serving the Lord? I found myself fighting with God who had become my adversary at that point. As soon as I broke through with God, I enjoyed complete victory and a joyous time despite the physical hardships. I had agreed with God concerning my situation and even if I had spent ten years in that cage, it would have made no difference. I was out of prison while yet in prison. The difference was that I realized that I was God's prisoner. What a place to be!

CHAPTER SEVEN

WITCHCRAFT

Larger snakes of different species will always eat smaller and weaker ones of another species when they lock in combat in a confined situation. This is a common natural phenomena and sheds light as to why the "serpent of Moses" was easily able to devour those of Pharaoh's magicians. God was showing His superior hand through His natural creation. This spectacular situation would not have been lost on the Egyptian leadership which reverenced certain serpents like the Egyptian cobra, one of the most powerful and deadliest of serpents.

When the magicians of Pharaoh stood before Moses to defy God, they were able to cast down their staves which turned into snakes as had the staff of Moses. The big difference however, was that the magicians performed their diabolic miracles by demonic enchantment. There are diabolic miracles and healings but they are not lasting, bring no peace of mind or spirit and bind a person to being satan's slave. The serpent of Moses gobbled up the serpents of the magicians. There came a point when the magicians could no longer perform and at that point, the enemy's power and hold over Egypt was broken and Goshen was freed.

At one time, one of my leading pastors had been a strong warlock. He could sit on a reed mat and fly two hundred miles in a night, kill someone and fly back again. People are deceived into thinking that the "Tales of the Arabian Nights" are simply "nice" fairy stories for children, especially since Walt Disney has cartooned them. No friends, they are true accounts of powerful demonic activity and not something which we should allow our children to watch. My ex-warlock pastor told me how he could change animals into different kinds of creatures by the diabolic powers invested in him. He also had the power to completely control even the most vicious of animals and often at night he would sleep with hyenas

and serpents protecting him. Hyenas would be his charioteers as these animals are often associated with witchcraft in Africa and greatly feared by the natives. Part of the reason for this is the ghoulish laughter that hyenas have.

The great Zulu king Shaka defeated a particularly wicked native queen, Nanquana. The punishment he inflicted upon her was to lock her in her royal hut with a hyena. Now the royal hut contained dozens of gleaming skulls of those whom Nanquana had defeated in battle. After each meal Shaka served her in captivity, the wicked queen would take down a skull, wipe some fat from her plate on it and cast it to the hyena. With its powerful jaws the hyena would crush and swallow all the bones. In this way, Nanquana was able to keep the hideous animal at bay for a couple of weeks. You see, the hyena is a cowardly creature and would not come for her as long as there was food it would not have to fight for. The time came however, when the skulls were all eaten and the hyena was hungry and tired of his diet of dry old bones. One night when she had fallen asleep from exhaustion he attacked and bit off her leg with just one bite of those powerful jaws. Nanquana sent word to Shaka requesting that he burn the hut so that *she* might die laughing at the hyena. Shaka granted her request on the grounds that an animal should not get the better over a human.

I well remember how the very jealous wife of one of the native pastors sought to kill her husband and myself. She visited a powerful witchdoctor who instructed her to bring a cage full of lizards. The woman diligently caught the lizards and returned with them to the witchdoctor. The man performed his many enchantments over both the woman and the lizards. Part of this ritual included the laceration of her flesh into which he poured some of his foul ointments. This gives him power over the body of his client. She then paid his outrageous fee and left with the lizards and her instructions. One night when the woman knew we were returning across the river and swamps she took the lizards down to the bank of the river where we normally landed and released them from the cage. As they crawled into the water they became fully grown, ferocious crocodiles. Those demonic creatures were especially assigned to grab us upon our return. The powers of darkness are able to achieve such incredibly diabolic

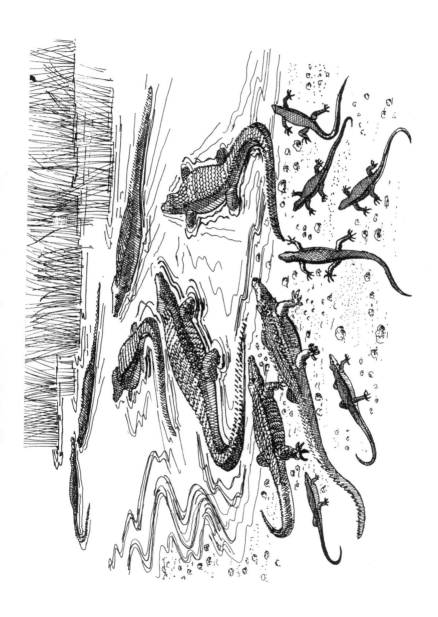

phenomena and the world is going to see more and more of these types of manifestations in the days ahead. This will include the werewolf of which horror movies have been made and the vampire and so on. The answer to these demonic manifestations is never to be afraid and run but rather to confront. Such demonic forces can have no power over us if we are walking in the power of God. In the situation of the lizards, they had been given our scent from some personal items so that they could "home in" on us. God gave us a warning of danger and orchestrated situations whereby we had to return a day earlier than we had expected. He directly instructed us to use a different landing area. At the time we did not know why but later on discovered what the woman had done. She was so amazed and frightened when she saw us arriving at the village. She realized that the power of God in us was greater than the power of darkness in the witchdoctor. She consulted him again but he confessed that if *that* power had failed to destroy us he had no further powers. Like the Egyptian magicians, he had come to the end of his abilities.

In Africa, the witches often catch bats and cast spells on them. They then direct them to fly into homes, especially the homes of Christian leaders where they hang from the rafters and begin to sow discord between husband and wife by interfering in conversation and twisting the meaning of speech. Before long couples begin to argue and fight where such situations had never before existed. This will often end up in the break-up of a Christian's home which is one of the prime targets of the devil in the church today.

Witchdoctors will also send snakes to people's homes. They slither around the house spitting and hissing but they are really speaking words of confusion and division, thereby creating disruption.

Believers cannot afford to take things at face value. We are commanded to "test" the spirits. In the United States some years ago, there was a woman "doing the rounds," as I say. The saddest thing was that she was highly endorsed by several "leading" ministers. Her particular fad was that she practiced stigmata. Oil and later blood would appear on her hands. It was a "sign" and everybody rushed to her to have her lay hands on them. Jesus said,

"A perverse and wicked generation seeketh after a sign." The intercessor for a major ministry so endorsed this woman that she went so far as to say that if anyone criticized her they would be severely judged by God. Well, I didn't have to meet the woman to know she was a witch. I didn't have to criticize her, I judged her according to the Word. She was later found to be a fraud. Sad to say, those same people who endorsed the witch were not held accountable for that endorsement. It seems to me that accountability in the Body of Christ extends only as far as sexual immorality and financial misconduct. Just as serious is the teaching of false doctrine. The perpetrators of the godless shepherding movement have never been held accountable! Oh yes, they apologized for their errors after creating years of havoc but they have never been made to account. The Word of God clearly declares that, *"If any man or angel preaches any other gospel let him be accursed."* Gal 1:8&9. Paul upbraided the Galatians for being "bewitched" in going back to the law. Gal 3:1.

The serpent is very subtle. I know of an organization which was totally infiltrated by the enemy. A young lady who looked like a frog, (she had the "toad" spirit) arrived at the ministry and was totally embraced by the leader. The leader had become somewhat fleshly and therefore was open to attack. Soon after this "toad" arrived at the headquarters there were manifestations of spirits and peculiar things began to happen. It was not long before the "toad" had sleazed her way into the inner workings of the ministry and become a favorite of the leader. Now, the leader had been given a chair as a gift and this had been placed in the office. Senior members on staff did not allow anyone to sit in this chair - it belonged to their "Boss." One day the "toad" demanded to have her photograph taken standing behind the chair with a couple of her friends. When the film was developed, there, seated in the chair was a clear image of a man - the "toad's" father! - as if he had actually been posing for the picture. I personally saw the photograph. Because of the speed of the shutter it had obviously picked up the spirit. The problem was that her father had died some two years earlier. The demon spirit or familiar (family) spirit was masquerading as her father. The "toad" loved that demon because it gave her influence and power. It was cast out of her but some nights later one of the other girls went down to the kitchen late at night to find the "toad" sitting in the middle of the floor asking the familiar spirit back. She had lost her "power" and wanted to regain it. Such conduct is no better than the behavior of the witches and warlocks in Africa.

In today's world we need to be particularly careful. There is so much happening in the supernatural spirit realm because creation is preparing for the coming of Jesus. Any manifestation of any person or spirit that does not glorify Jesus or line up with the Word of God should not only be considered suspect but a lie. Recent appearances of "Mary" with accompanying phenomena are very questionable to me because the so-called voice of Mary which is interpreted through a priest does not emphatically command the Romans to worship Jesus. Many reputable Christian writers are endorsing such phenomena. I believe their endorsement comes from their own deception in the erroneous idea that there will be one ecumenical church in the last days. Rome already claims such a thing BUT there is already a universal church: one body of believers! It is that body which comes directly under the headship of the Lord Jesus Christ.

There is a realm of "Christian Witchcraft," if we may call it such. Christians who operate in the soul realm to manipulate and control and obtain things are as much into witchcraft as those witchdoctors in Africa. Let me illustrate with a couple of clear examples.

One of these spiritual "flakes" as I call them, arrived in Africa. She had an incredible testimony of how God had healed her from cancer and used this to get into churches. Everybody fell over themselves to have her speak and teach but I was neither impressed with the woman nor did I want her around me. She gave me the "creeps." My spiritual antenna was signaling **"DANGER."** It is very difficult to be the odd man out at times but I would rather go with my intuition than with the opinions of men. This "flake" flew off to Maputo, the capital of Mocambique to visit the then President Samora Machel. She returned gushing that she had given him a Bible and he had received Jesus. What garbage! Machel no more received Christ than did Hitler or Stalin and he features in the same category as they.

Some years later I was traveling on the East Coast and preaching in New Hampshire. The pastor had an Indian friend staying with him. During the course of conversation he asked if I knew...... (the "flake"). I affirmed and wondered which way the discussion was going to turn. "Well, what do you think of the lady?" He questioned.

"I have some reservations," I cautiously replied. "My spirit is very disturbed when she's around but most people think she's wonderful."

"I'll tell you a story," he said. "You'll probably think I'm crazy but this is the truth of the matter.

'I had a friend who was a wealthy businessman. All he ever wanted to do was pastor a church. When time came for him to retire, he sold his business and bought a church building. He built up a congregation of about seventy and it was a good, solid church with a lot of love but the people were very naive. I don't know how, but this woman was invited to speak for three days. Incredible things happened from the moment of her arrival. The pastor and his wife began bickering where this had never happened before in their marriage.'"

"Yes, I know what you mean. The witches in Africa send bats to disrupt the home and it seems that something similar happened here," I said.

"'The next thing that happened was that the woman wanted to go shopping. The pastor took her out and said that he felt *compelled* to buy her whatever she wanted. By the end of three days he had spent almost $10,000 on her. The last evening she spoke they took up a final offering for her and out of that small church she walked away with another $10,000. People said they had felt *compelled* to give. Now, here's the key,'" he declared. "'Arriving back at the house after her departure, the pastor found that she had left her briefcase behind. Upon opening it to try to obtain a forwarding address, some books on the practice of witchcraft fell out. Instantly the pastor knew what had transpired over the last three days. A few hours later the woman called and was firmly told by the Indian's friend, 'I know what you are. Your briefcase is in the dumpster with the books. You will never again return to this church.' The woman became very nasty and said, 'I'll show you,

you'll pay for this.' And pay he did. It was the next day when his wife opened their safe that they found all their cash was gone. The money had disappeared but only the pastor and his wife knew the combination. The very next week the pastor was dead. It was sudden. There appeared to be nothing wrong with him.'"

"That's pure witchcraft, African style. She must have picked some of it up there," I declared. But this happened in Christian America! Such a person is operating in the power of the soul from purely selfish motives.

We have a "money snake" in Africa. This is a real snake that is taken by a client to a witchdoctor where a spell is cast on it. At this point the snake actually changes its form and takes on a triangular shape. It is demonized and hypnotized to "eat" money. Such a snake will not only smell out the money belonging to those to whom it has been assigned but will also be able to get into the money no matter where it is. A locked briefcase or safe is no guarantee against the money snake. Such a creature will slip in, literally swallow the money whether notes, coins or both and slither out again. After it has eaten its fill, it returns to the witchdoctor and vomits up its entire load. The witchdoctor takes his percentage and gives the rest to his client. The snake will return only to the witchdoctor who has the power over it.

One night a group of pastors was asleep in a mud hut. The money snake decided to visit them as my overseer was carrying salaries for other pastors. The snake slipped in through the window but fell on to the bed of the overseer and became entangled in the sheets. The man leapt up screaming and shouting. Confusion reigned. Soon, a flaming torch was brought. In the meanwhile, the snake had extricated itself from the sheets and stood erect almost to the tip of its tail, with eyes a fire. The pastor spoke to it directly, "Tonight I am going to kill you, you devil!" Very quickly, the creature turned to slip back out through the window but the pastor attacked, beating it with a stick and breaking its back. It is very interesting to note that the demonized snake seemed to understand when the Pastor conversed with it. Several of the pastors then beat the vile thing to death. It was perfectly triangular in shape. Once killed, a money snake cannot be cut open as the stench is so nauseating that a person cannot eat for days and will spend many

days vomiting, sometimes even to death. An incredible fury was unleashed against that overseer by the witchdoctor for killing the snake. He knew exactly what had happened to his snake through the information chain that the demonic realm had set up. In the same way that demons relayed the information to the witchdoctor so also did demons relay the news of Israel's crossing of the Red Sea and conquest of Pharaoh to all the Canaanites who instantly became afraid. (Ex 15:14-16). *"The people shall hear and be afraid: sorrow shall take hold on the inhabitants of Palestina. Then the dukes of Edom shall be amazed; the mighty men of Moab, trembling shall take hold upon them; all the inhabitants of Canaan shall melt away. Fear and dread shall fall upon them; by the greatness of thine arm they shall be as still as a stone; till thy people pass over, O Lord, till the people pass over, which thou hast purchased."* The next day whilst preaching, a small but deadly scorpion dropped on to the shoulder of the overseer and stung him on the neck. Almost instantly he lost consciousness and was in a critical condition for several days. Praise God for the power of prayer which delivered him from death and raised him up. Once again the power of the enemy was thwarted and his sting of death overcome.

I know of a certain ministry which coveted an adjacent piece of real estate. For many years the owner would not sell. Now that ministry works by witchcraft to literally control the movement and thinking of its members. This is no different at all to what happened with Jim Jones and his cult. The leader of the ministry "siced" (the expression he used when giving testimony) his sister on the owner of that real estate. The owner was *"compelled"* to sell it against his will. Now people applauded the "workings of God" in that situation not knowing any better because Christians can be so naive. First, the commandments tell us not to covet and second, God is fair and generous and He certainly does not manipulate. It was with the power of witchcraft that the ministry obtained the land. In fact, they plundered and stole it. It is the serpent who robs, steals and destroys. This is exactly what happened to Eve in the garden. Never resort to soul manipulation and control to gain advantage over people.

Never, never get into the soul realm and operate in the flesh. The moment the soul realm is subjected to the lower order of nature of the flesh a person is carnal and can easily operate under the influence of strong demon spirits. With a veneer of Christianity, your operation always looks good and plausible. The reason why people can get away with such behavior is because most Christians have little or no discernment or alternatively, there are corrupt, selfish, motives which lead them into being willingly seduced.

Saul deliberately opened himself to demons because he was jealous and bitter towards David. Instead of resisting the enemy, Saul became his direct agent and ended up visiting the witch at Endor whom he was, by law, obliged to put to death. Many times, Christians become direct agents of satan.

For twelve years I worked in covenant relationship with some precious people. They learned with time, how to become financially independent in the ministry which is wonderful but they soon became jealous and coveted total leadership positions. I released them to establish their own ministry. They quickly undermined my own authority and position and it was not long before my familiar friends had wittingly or (I prefer to believe) unwittingly given themselves to be used of the serpent to destroy both myself and the ministry. For three years I went through a living hell. I experienced wave after wave of attack which came from their quarter as they tried to utterly annihilate me. What was worse was that they had been "inside traders" knowing the very ways in which I both thought and operated. Maybe the serpent had once been an "inside trader" with Adam and Eve. He was subtle then and is just as subtle today. Time which ought to be spent in developing the Kingdom is consumed with fighting witchcraft. Such witchcraft emanates from the soul realm of dissatisfied, disillusioned and dangerously jealous Christians who send volleys of missiles against you.

If you are manipulated or controlled by any person and have neither the stamina nor moral fortitude to confront the person, then break off the relationship immediately. I never cease to be amazed at how the ruling demons in a person know when they are about to be confronted. I had a "she witch" who wheedled her way into the ministry through her husband. He was totally different when she was not around and the first time he had worked with us in the field he had been traveling with a friend and was reliable and acceptable. This all changed when his wife arrived. The woman knew exactly what buttons to press to get her husband fired up and then exactly how to calm him down. In such fashion, she controlled him and everyone around because his outbursts, hitherto unseen, were most unpleasant. Each time I decided to confront that spirit in her she completely changed and became humble and submissive until the "danger period" was over. Then she would revert to her previous behavioral pattern.

Demons can take on multitudes of characteristics but we must not be deceived. I have seen demons whimper like beaten children and beg not to be hurt. I have seen demons make people look as if they have been abused and misused. Then too, I have witnessed the "macho" demon which can break fetters and chains and throw four strong men a considerable distance. I remember many years ago evangelizing in Eastern Zimbabwe where, in a farm compound I found a brother and sister who were so bound by strong demons that they were chained to a tree inside a locked cage. Those frail looking nine year olds could throw large men and pin them down. Without their heavy fetters the whole village was terrorized by them. As soon as I arrived on the scene those demons acted as lambs because they knew their time of control had ended.

CHAPTER EIGHT

CURSINGS

In Africa, perhaps the most common statement I have ever heard is, "Pastor we are a cursed people." I have heard this declaration from both rich and poor, educated and uneducated, saved and unsaved and from different tribes and different nations. What a tragic and negative confession which has enslaved a whole continent. God never cursed Adam or Eve. He cursed the serpent. He could not curse that which was created in His image.

How different are the Jewish people, who at least every Friday evening at their Shabat meal declare the blessings of Abraham upon their families and remember the promise of God Himself in Gen 12:3. *"I will bless them that bless thee and curse him that curseth thee: and in thee shall all the families of the earth be blessed."* If you are a Jew hater you had better repent and change because you will never prosper. Americans particularly had better be thankful to the Jews for it was a Jewish banker in Philadelphia, Hiam Solomon, who gave the necessary finances which caused the tide to be turned in favor of Washington at Valley Forge. In thankfulness to Solomon, George Washington placed the Star of David over the Eagle and the Menorah of Israel on the dollar bill. Many Christians curse the Jews for crucifying Christ. **WRONG!** Christ Himself declared that, *"No man taketh my life from me."* Jn 10:18. Christ freely laid down His own life because of sin, the curse of which He broke. Men such as Haamen, Hitler and Stalin were all Jew haters who died raving lunatics and will one day stand before a **Jewish King** and give account. Now Proverbs 18:21 declares that the "Power of life and death is in the tongue." I wonder why the serpent has a forked tongue and can only hiss when at one time he spoke to Eve? I believe that just as he was cursed by God to go on his belly and eat dust, so his tongue was also cursed. He cannot now speak intelligibly. Take the human tongue and merely clip a small "V" in the tip and a person is no longer able to speak comprehensibly. James declares in Ja.3:6 *"And the tongue is a fire, a world of iniquity: so is the tongue among our members, that it defileth the whole body and setteth on fire the course of nature and is **set on fire of hell.**"*

People need to be very careful of how they talk. Christians should be people of blessing who bless others instead of cursing. James continues in Ja 3:8 that the tongue is an *"Unruly evil, full of deadly poison."* It is amazing that the saliva of the spitting cobra is deadly poisonous to the eyes and the bite deadly to the body. Have you ever seen an infuriated Christian? The tongue of such a person which blesses God one moment can then pronounce the vilest curses with such fury that they literally spit out a deadly poison. In my last chapter, I mentioned about a ministry which coveted real estate and another ministry which was controlled by a "toad" spirit operating through familiar spirits. Common to both ministries is strong bondage made effective through cursings. Anyone who tried to leave those ministries was cursed. I have known numerous people who have finally mustered up the courage to leave after years of misery and have been cursed by the leadership as they left. In most cases the women leaving, were cursed to be barren "spiritually" for the rest of their lives. Such have ended up barren, physically, having miscarriage or having to undergo hysterectomies or have cysts removed because their female organs were affected by such a curse. That's pure witchcraft and it operates in the church.

If someone has pronounced a curse over you, make sure that you break that thing and put it under the Blood of Jesus and then place the Blood of Jesus between you and whoever pronounced the curse. In Gen 31:32 *With whomsoever thou findest thy gods, let him not live: For Jacob knew not that Rachel had stolen them. Jacob, in foolish, rash speech cursed his own beloved Rachel who died in childbirth.* Gen 35:16-19 *And it came to pass, as her soul was in departing, [for she died] that she called his name Benoni: but his father called him Benjamin.* Rachel was unable to stop the curse from becoming effective because she was under a self inflicted curse through stealing according to Zech 5:3 which declares, *"For everyone that stealeth shall be cut off....."* Her problem was compounded because she had taken her father's idols and reaped God's curse declared in Deut 27:15. *Cursed be the man that maketh any graven or molten image, an abomination unto the Lord.* Idols are not merely images of wood or stone. They may well be your favorite preacher or tele-evangelist. In certain Christian circles people have their "gurus" whose word is absolute even when it contradicts THE Word. That's idolatry. When we begin to deify a human and see no wrong in him or his activity, it is idolatry. Friend, if you have idols or images in your home or life you are directly under the curse of the Almighty and the enemy has a legal right to plunder your home, your family and your storehouse. Start to be obedient to God according to Deut 28:2-14 *And all these blessings shall come on thee, and shall overtake thee, if thou shalt harken to the voice of the Lord they God..........* Unless we forsake evil and rebellion we can never prosper no matter how much we declare blessings with our mouth. The two go hand-in-hand: to obey and to declare blessings will bring forth fruit.

Remember, there are those, so-called Christians who curse and manipulate and control and who appear to and do prosper. I want to tell you that the devil can cause people and his agents to prosper *for a season.* The serpent promised the kingdoms of this world to Christ if Christ would bow down to him. One preacher said that satan is a liar and the kingdoms were not his to give. Oh yes they were and are until he is finally cast into the Lake of Fire. Only then will the Kingdoms of this World become the Kingdoms of our Lord and of His Christ. If you are into "Christian witchcraft" and cursing you will reap what you sow. Repent of your controlling, manipulating and plundering and receive God's blessings. There are many who have operated in this fashion for so long that they no longer have a conscience with regard to their lust and greed.

Perhaps some of the strongest curses which allow the serpent to create havoc in a person's life are the generational curses. Ex 20:3-5, *"And thou shalt have no other gods before me. Thou shalt not make unto thee any graven image, or any likeness of any thing that is in heaven above, or that is in the earth beneath, or that is in the water under the earth: Thou shalt not bow down thyself to them, nor serve them: for I the Lord thy God am a jealous God, visiting the iniquity of the fathers upon the children unto the third and fourth generation of them that hate me."* expressly commands that man is to make no brazen or molten image of anything created for the purpose of bowing down to worship. The curse for such is unto the fourth generation or one hundred and sixty years and God declares that making an image to worship is hated of Him. The blessings of the Lord endure to a thousand generations.

So many people travel the nations and think it's cute to buy curios and images of African warriors or brass statues of Buddha or masks, only to find that their homes are in turmoil and they begin to inherit a curse instead of a blessing. If in doubt about things in your home, get rid of them. Many people have said, "Oh, but it doesn't hurt; it's only a Buddha door stop...." or "It means nothing to *me*...." Well, it means everything to God.

My mother told me that my deceased grandfather was deep into freemasonry. He had an image of the freemason pyramid and eye hanging on the wall in the living room; you know the very same one that appears on the U.S. one dollar bill. Mom recounts how they were often terrorized by the eye as it really came alive and followed them around the room. Well, demonic influences can enter through something like that. The generational curse which came with that Masonic demon is gambling, drinking and demonic activity. That curse has now been broken by the Blood of Jesus over our family. Only Jesus can bring complete freedom. He broke every curse of the serpent at the Cross of Calvary. If you are under a generational curse then take it to the Cross and have it broken by the Blood. It may also need a man of God to pray strong prayers of deliverance over you to break those bondages of generational curses. Never let your grandfather or father "pray over you" or "bless" you before they die unless it is the blessings of the Lord Jesus Christ. Anything else will perpetuate generational curses.

People are very proud that things have been in their family for generations not knowing that such things can be curses and not blessings. Never receive heirlooms, no matter how valuable, unless you are absolutely sure they are not bringing a curse or bondage with them. If there is a requirement to fulfill certain conditions or behave in a certain way as part of the inheritance, then tell them thanks but to keep the inheritance or heirloom. It is

better to incur family wrath and lose what they have to offer than to open up yourself and your family to a generational curse.

Just because some tradition has been done in the family, "For as long as we can remember," makes it more wrong than right. "Oh it's harmless, just a nice little tradition," you say. Yes, like Halloween which is totally demonic. Many people don't realize that their nice little tradition is a generational curse which keeps them from serving God and makes them slaves to demons or keeps them under the control of someone else. The Word declares, *"If the Son therefore shall make you free, you shall be free indeed"* Jn 8:36.

People in the occult always pass on the generational curse by both giving an image and praying their curses over their children and grandchildren. The powers invested in the one are transferred to the other. This is called "Transference of Powers," and brings spiritual darkness, bondage and misery. When the blessings of God are bestowed upon the next generation by men and women of God, we never talk about, "Transference of Powers," but of "Transferring the Anointing," which comes from the Lord and brings light, life and freedom.

I remember as a young boy; not only encountering demons at night but actually being caught up by those hideous creatures and being tossed from one to another. It was always, "Just another bad dream!" No it was not - I was really encountering strong powers of darkness which I believe, came from that Masonic generational curse. Thank God, Jesus saved me and broke that chain. Who knows that I might have become involved in the occult if it was not for freedom in Christ? The devil certainly made a strong bid for my life but his powers are broken. Thank God for a family that is becoming saved, one by one and for the generational curses and traditions which are being smashed. Only the Blood of Jesus can deliver and set free. There are generational curses over cities, towns and entire nations. The continent of Africa is under the generational curse of Ham and that's one hundred generations now. It does not have to be like that: the power of the curse can be broken at any time just as long as we're not going to hang on to the traditions that go with it. Jesus said, *"You make the Word of God of none effect through your tradition"* Mk 7:13.

Let me conclude the chapter with a final illustration. In 1959 Lake Kariba was built on the Zambezi River in Southern Rhodesia. It was the biggest man made lake of that era. The native peoples maintained that the Zambezi River god was displeased with the infringement of his freedom. The peoples had been bound by strong witchcraft for generations. It is no wonder they live in bondage and poverty, but visitors think their traditions are "nice." The Zambezi River god, Nyaminyami is in the image of a huge curled serpent and is pure evil. However, people believe it is just fine to buy a soap-stone carving of the hideous image as memorabilia from their vacation, not even realizing that such souvenirs are made by witchdoctors or at the very least cursed by them.

A woman in Malawi was attacked by a python which curled around her in the same fashion as Nyaminyami is curled. The woman had very little choice as to what she could do to save herself. She grabbed that serpent by the head and literally bit clean through its neck until she had completely severed the head. It was the only thing she could do to save herself.

Artifacts are often transported across the world to bring generational curses into the homes of the purchaser or recipient. Before Jacob led his family back into Canaan he made them clean out their idols. It is time to clean out your homes. America in particular is notorious for collecting all kinds of "antique" bric-a-brac. It is nothing but garbage which clutters the walls, floors, windows and rooms. Naively, people bring into their homes the "cursed thing" which has been procured at some garage sale or some Amish store. It is time to clean out the idols and you will find that simple living, uncluttered and uncomplicated with "things" is the best environment for both the Lord and yourself.

Anyway, I knew a lady who not only brought the hideous image of Nyaminyami but also a mask. From the moment those things arrived in her home everything that could go wrong went wrong. The husband and wife began to argue and fight, furniture began to move supernaturally (it's called apports and is demonic activity) and the whole home began to break up. The wife called her Christian mother-in-law for help and this Godly woman rushed down to spend a week with her children. One afternoon as she was alone in the house, she happened to sit opposite the newly acquired mask. She let out a gasp as a pair of "real" eyes glared at her from the mask. They were evil and demonic. As soon as her daughter-in-law returned the mask and the Zambezi River god were taken from the house and burned. The curse was broken over the home and immediately things began to return to normal.

It is not worth playing with the powers of the occult. Such things are serious and can rob us of our eternity with God. I have an aunt whose attitude is, "I've always been like that and I'm not going to change," and an uncle who says that when he dies he just wants to join his father whether it be heaven or hell. If hell is good enough for his father then it will be good enough for him. They are very bound to family traditions and romanticizing about past glories of the family. That is pure stupidity: Masonic bondage of slavery to alcohol, slavery to social demands and slavery to gambling which lost our family great wealth in the past, is realism and not glory. It's generational curse and not freedom.

Thank God that I'm out of it and living for Jesus and not in the past; a slave to illusion. You need to get out of your past too if you are in any way a slave to it. If others do not want to leave with you go alone!

CHAPTER NINE

DELIVERANCE

It is very important to understand that we are tripartite beings consisting of Spirit, Soul and body. Diagrammatically it can be present thus:

GOD

⇑

God Conscious	Intuition	Knowledge
	SPIRIT	

Mind	Emotion	Will
	SOUL	

Nourish	Defend	Reproduce
	BODY	

⇓

SATAN

The real character of any person is their soul. The soul is the battleground between the body and the spirit. The spirit was "breathed" into us from conception and comes directly from God. It is that Divine breath which causes a thirst in man for a relationship with Him. The body is the element of physical flesh which, to put it simply, is the vessel for the soul and spirit.

Now, we must understand that there is a complex inter-relationship of the three; an overlapping which produces "gray" areas in our lives. It is for this reason that it is difficult to simplify problem areas in a person's life and to know the real details about demon possession and oppression. It is important however, not to get bound with technological arguments but to know that such issues are real and can be overcome with the power of the Blood of Jesus and the word of our authority.

SOUL

This is the realm of the real personality and is the battleground between spirit and body. We often talk of the soul as being the heart, but this is wrong. The two important factors in the soul area of our lives is emotion and will. It must be remembered that our emotions were given to us by God: the ability to laugh, be sad, get excited and so on. But, when the emotions are dominating a person's life, that person is soulish. Soul control can be the most manipulative, subtly dominating fact in a person's life and nothing is worse or more miserable than a person with corrupt emotions. I have used the term "soulish" but in actual fact, someone ruled by the soul or flesh is carnal according to Paul the Apostle.

Corrupted emotions cause one to be a slave in a macabre play acting out a part for the benefit of a manipulated audience. The problem is that an emotional wreck will always look for scapegoats and never take responsibility for self. It is through the slavery of emotions that soul control arises. For there to be any form of soul control it is required that one person is able to lord it over another: a dominant character and a dominated character. Both mutually feed off the strengths and weaknesses of the other and a sick so-dependency arises. Somebody who is in the habit of throwing temper tantrums will rule because others are afraid to confront the issue.

The corruption of the soul took place at the fall. It was Eve's soul realm that the serpent attacked, playing on her emotions and persuading her that she would become as god knowing good and evil. Indeed, having eaten of the forbidden fruit her eyes *were* opened. No doubt, for the first time, she knew how to manipulate and seduce with her emotion, the first victim being her husband.

Now, when the will is a slave to the flesh a person will fulfill the lusts of the flesh but when the will is subject to the spirit the emotions will be in right perspective. The situation is not, "how I feel" but "what is God's will?" I will subject myself to the will of God.

A person who allows his mind thoughts to be dominated by the flesh, the world and satan will enslave his whole being. Paul writing to both the Ephesians and Galatians teaches that life consists of habits. There are good habits and bad habits. People are creatures of habit. We are commanded to put on the mind of Christ; to let this mind be in you which was also in Christ, thou wilt keep him in perfect peace whose mind is stayed on thee. What Paul teaches is that we need to put off bad habit pattern and replace them with good habit patterns. When does a thief cease being a thief? Most people would say when he stops stealing. Wrong! A thief stops being a thief when his total habit changes: when he ceases to steal and begins to live honestly, working and paying his way. When does an adulterer cease being such? When he stops having illicit sex. Wrong! Proof of real change is when the adulterer settles down to honest righteous living with his or her spouse and ceases frequenting places and situations of compromise.(even in thought because that is also the will.)

BODY

God created the body as a vessel for the spirit and the soul. Of itself though, the body does three things: it must nourish itself, defend itself and reproduce itself. This is common to all natural bodies whether human, animal, reptile or plant. It would be very foolish to stand idly by and let a man blatantly stab you without doing something to defend yourself. To do nothing - unless you have a clear word from God - is not spiritual but foolish.

When the emotions begin to rule the soul it has a direct effect on the body. Under emotional turmoil, nourishment turns to gluttony or bizarre eating behavior such as anorexia. Defense becomes war so that there are Christians who are continuously aggressive and thrive in contention and finally, natural reproduction becomes physical license and sexual immorality.

Now, the problem with most people is that they look for an escape mechanism. Unfortunately today, that escape mechanism has become the word, "deliverance." Every lazy, carnal Christian rushes to the altar to have hands layed upon them to cast out a non-existent devil. The problem is **FLESH.** Now, there may well be a point where a person has so opened their life that they have, in fact, become possessed with a demon. For the most part however, Christians have fallen into bad habit patterns and it takes supreme strength and hard work to crawl out of the gutter. Many a believer has become disillusioned because they feel the same on Monday morning as they felt the night before when they were supposed to be delivered.

The prophet Zechariah declares, *"Deliver **THYSELF**, O Zion, that dwellest with the daughter of Babylon."* It is within the power of most people to make a decision to fulfill the will of God and begin to walk in it. There are some of course, whose minds are not free and who have no will of their own because they are completely under the domination of satan. I remember pastoring in a certain city. A lady who attended the church had many problems. She always told me how rotten her husband was. Now when anyone does that to me, the first thing I want to do is to meet the rotten partner. Well eventually I met this "rotten" husband only to find him most charming and presentable. We became friends but he would never receive Christ. After sometime, I realized the man was not free to make a decision because his mind was veiled and his will was controlled. I laid hands on him one evening breaking the powers of darkness over him. Instantly he began to fully understand God's salvation plan and made a commitment to Christ. Most people however, need to shake themselves and rise up to deliver themselves from slothful habits that have placed them in bondage to the soul or flesh. It is time to decide, "I will obey God's will and do what is right." Such decision means turning away from sin, breaking old habit patterns and may even require breaking certain relationships with people who have soul-controlled you for years. Oh the bliss of freedom.

I do not believe that it is necessary for a person to pour out the most intimate details of their lives to someone in the "deliverance" ministry. Actually, I am tired of deliverance, inner-healing, prayer cleansing and all the fancy names by which a person gets access into the private areas of people's lives and then holds them to ransom. Just how many times must a person be delivered, healed or prayer-cleansed so as to get free?

True deliverance is casting devils out of those who are really possessed or oppressed. For the most part, people need to know how to break soul relationships for which I have outlined a prayer below. The relationship between David and Jonathan was made in heaven and worked because both of them had an incredible relationship with God. One thing is absolutely certain: if our relationship with God is out of sync then so will be our relationship with one another. In the same fashion, if our relationship with one another is off then our relationship with God will be out of balance. Many people are striving to walk in victory with God when they are not walking in victory with each other and wonder why there is no spiritual progress.

PRAYER

Lord Jesus, I recognize that I am in a soul tie or soul relationship with...................(name person, thing or place). I know this is sin. I ask you to forgive me this sin which has exalted....................above You. I now place your Blood, Lord Jesus, between myself and ....as I renounce this soul tie. Set me free Lord Jesus. Satan, I address myself to you in the name of Jesus. I close every door and avenue to you now in this affair. I break the powers I have given to you in this relationship between ....and me. I put the Blood of Jesus between me and you satan. You have no more place in my life. I choose that you leave me alone. I choose to be free. I choose to break this soul control now in Jesus' name.

I ask you Lord to protect me and cover me in Your Blood as you release me from this prison of soul bondage. Thank you Jesus for setting me free.

Such a simple prayer will have a powerful impact upon your life if you are soul controlled. Such a prayer will bring instant release and freedom but it is then absolutely necessary to walk out that freedom and this can come only through the cross.

The soul controlled person will be very familiar with such phrases as; "If you love me you will....." for manipulating somebody to do something that may not be right for them. "Nobody understands," for when they want you to feel sorry for them.

Each statement and many more are designed to manipulate emotions and bring control. If you're under such bondage or have been told that to leave this person or ministry you will be in rebellion is enough for you to put on your running shoes and flee.

The saddest thing of all is that innocent, sincere Christians who know very little are manipulated because of their pure motive to serve God and their fear of displeasing Him. The moment anyone tells you that you should not leave because of displeasing God, it is your cue to leave. God alone may have the prerogative to tell us He is displeased with us for whatever reason.

SPIRIT

It is that part of us which is God conscious and divides us from the rest of creation. When the spirit of a man is not fired by God and fed from Heaven, then such a man is no better than the animals. This was ably illustrated by King Nebuchadnezzar from whom the spirit departed. He became like an animal to the extent of eating grass and walking on all fours. It was only into man that God breathed His Spirit of life. Now Paul urges the Ephesians to, "Grow up into Him in all things." The Word declares that the whole of creation is groaning and travailing for the manifestation of the sons of God. Who are the sons of God? Those who are totally obedient to, and led by the Holy Spirit. This means that such a person walks in constant communion with God and their will is completely submitted to the will and desire of the Holy Spirit. This is not impossible though to one who is carnal, it might appear so. It is God's will that all His people live and walk in the spirit and they will not thereby fulfill the lusts of the flesh. The spirit and the flesh are enmity: that which is of the spirit gives life but the flesh profits nothing.

It is apparently clear then, that there is a place for real deliverance when a person is overcome with devils. In my experience most real possession comes through direct involvement with the occult whether of the individual or through generational curses. Some people who have so opened their lives to sin may also be possessed or at least plagued by devils. Then, there are those who, because of a high calling of God are specifically assigned for destruction by the devil who sends volleys against such. Under each of these situations we have authority in the name of Jesus. People who dabble in sin and come under demonic attack need only to change their life-style, become obedient to God, resist the devil and he will flee.

Apart from genuine cases of demonic possession or oppression most other issues are strong soul control or fleshly carnality. For the latter, what is required is honest repentance and some clean holy living.

It is long overdue that Christians would rise up to be giants in the land and put to flight the works of the enemy.

CHAPTER TEN

THE INVASION OF PLANET EARTH

My final chapter is a warning and designed to enlighten people as to what is taking place on this planet. The serpent has never changed tactics. Actually the devil is not at all original but people are too de-sensitized to realize it. That old serpent, satan and the devil is going about *as* a roaring lion seeking whom he may devour. Just as he is not a lion, so he is not an angel of light.

The devil is preparing for his final onslaught against humanity, knowing he has but a short time to live. One night I had a vision in which I stood on a plain similar to that described in chapter one. I could hear this cacophony of sound - screaming, moaning and agonizing - echoing and re-echoing across the plain. In the distance I saw the biggest Caterpillar ever imaginable; frighteningly enormous. The blades of the Cat were so long I could not see the ends of them. The Cat itself was so big that it would have reached six or seven stories of a building. The engine droned with incredible power, pushing vast amounts of debris towards me. As I came closer, I realized that the debris being pushed along were multitudes of people, each of them still alive. Some were trying to climb the blade but kept slipping down while others were trying to rush ahead of the blade and many were fighting each other or tramping each other under foot. There was complete chaos and pandemonium. Suddenly I saw this vast crevice in the earth. It looked something like the Grand Canyon but there was no bottom to it and it was completely dark. The Cat pushed that mass of humanity towards the enormous fissure. People were screaming and plunging over the edge. Some people tried to hang on to the blade, others grabbed at roots which protruded from the sides of the walls. Shrieks of high pitched laughter came from the driver's seat - and who was the driver? Satan, that old serpent himself! He was delighted as multitudes

were being plunged into eternal darkness. He jumped up and down with glee behind the controls of the Cat as he maneuvered the machine until every last person was forced over the edge and into the bottomless pit.

The devil is invading the earth and we are going to see more and more manifestations of his power on this planet. Recently, in the nation of Tanzania, there have been demons masquerading as people. Several testimonies have been coming in from churches about how some "young men" and women have fallen in love and married. On their wedding nights brides have testified that their new "husbands" revealed their true identity for the first time. On climbing into bed they showed themselves to have hooves for feet. They then violated their brides and disappeared. Genesis declares, *"That the sons of God saw the daughters of men that they were fair; and they took them wives of all which they chose."* (Gen 6:2). The nations, especially in the Western World, are being seduced and deceived into accepting the "abnormal" as normal. I touched on this in the second chapter with regard to "E.T." Planet Earth is being invaded by superior creatures from outer space. Give me a break! Do I believe in Martians? **NO!** But I certainly believe in demons and in fallen angels and these creatures definitely can and do take on different forms. In the West, everything that is hideous and abnormal is imposed upon society as normal or "cute." Children are told from the earliest age that their deformed, mentally retarded contemporaries are normal. No they are not! I am not saying that we should not love them or accept them but they are not normal. Why? Because in most cases they are the product of sinful behavioral patterns of the parents. A woman who smokes, takes drugs and drinks whilst pregnant is not only violating her own body but also the fruit of her womb. A violated body is not normal and when born the fruit often is not normal. Under Levitical law a deformed human was under no circumstances permitted to be in priesthood or even enter the presence of God. Praise God that under the Blood all are now permitted to enter into the presence of God but it still does not make the deformed normal.

Now you say that's harsh. No, it's truthful and realistic. The day has already come to the West, where to think differently from the rest of society is to be a threat to normal patterns of decency and behavior. Now, precious few people ever want to be out of step with mass opinion; it is secure to follow the crowd. So, when mass opinion says that dinosaurs are cute and nice we accept it. When mass opinion said that Hitler was a good fellow, it was accepted. When mass opinion will say that the Anti-Christ is here for the betterment of the world, he will be acceptable. When mass opinion will state that every demonically, satanically violated human, animal, reptile and insect which gives rise to hideously possessed creatures are normal, they will be accepted. In today's world, a Goliath would not only be acceptable but totally embraced as perhaps - a basket ball hero? Think about it! The frightening outcome of what I am saying is that the only dissenting voices are those Bible believing, Holy Ghost Christians who stand for their faith and for what is right according to God's Word and His opinion. Such are going to be termed, "abnormal," "violators," and the "social threats," the "scum and offscouring of the earth," to be imprisoned, beheaded, interned and fit only for annihilation or slavery. This is exactly what the prophet said when they would call evil good and good evil.

Why has this crazy reversal of normal and abnormal taken place? Simply because the liberal, anti-God, anti-Christ educators and media moguls of society have become the tools of satanically inspired men who are imposing their views on a gullible world. Americans have become the least free thinking people on the planet. That's why it is hard for them to accept this chapter and in fact, this book. The whole planet is being prepared for a mighty invasion as happened in the days of Noah before the great flood. That is why every perverted sex maniac, mass murderer and social misfit is put in prison to be reformed at tax payer's expense only to be released after a short while to return to their perverted ways and terrorize society. Why is it that the law-makers are powerless? They have planned it so. The take-over of society has begun in earnest.

When werewolves and giants roam the streets and hideously possessed people, deformed by sin and satan, are given equal if not preferential rights, they will be embraced as "cute." Rev.9:7-11 *"And the shapes of the locusts were like unto horses prepared unto battle; and on their heads were as it were crowns like gold, and their faces were as the faces of men. And they had hair as the hair of women, and their teeth were as the teeth of lions. And they had breastplates, as it were breastplates of iron; and the sound of their wings was as the sound of chariots of many horses running to battle. And they had tails like unto scorpions, and there were stings in their tails: and their power was to hurt men five months. And they had a king over them, which is the angle of the bottomless pit, whose name in the Hebrew tongue is Abaddon, but in the Greek tongue hath his name Apollyon.*" And, when the mark of the beast comes, multitudes will willingly accept it for fear of being out-of-step with their friends and society. Better to be out-of-step with the world and public opinion than out-of-step with God.

The world believes the age-old lie that a real, living God to whom I must pay allegiance is an affront to my intelligence. How sick man has become to believe we came from ameba or evolved from an ape or gorilla. Man was made in the express image of God and was given dominion over the rest of creation. That old serpent continues to perpetrate his original lie that if we eat of knowledge we shall be as gods, knowing good and evil. No, we become slaves to the vain imaginations of men who are full of sin, pride and rebellion. The devil's master plan to take over the world is in place. Men have believed his lie and have willfully become his tools. Every misfit, pervert, sin loving, violent maniac whom we are told is normal but needs only a little love and understanding will soon rule under the directorship of the world system. The Church will be the number one enemy of the state just as it is the number one enemy of the serpent.

Everybody who has read this please get **REAL**. It is not time to hide in fear but a time to rise up. If you have never received Christ, receive Him and then rise up and be who God wants you to be. Don't be afraid of demons, the devil, the perverts, the world system or the anti-Christ.

It is given to dynamic Holy Ghost men and women to terrorize and torment the world system, the anti-Christ system. Become a Holy Ghost terrorist today according to Rev. 11:10 "And they that dwell upon the earth shall rejoice over them, and make merry, and shall send gifts one to another; because these two prophets tormented them that dwelt on the earth." It is given to us to torment and frustrate the devil AND those men who are in alliance with him and who oppose God and His will. Quit using the excuse that you were violated and molested as a child or you have had a raw deal in life. Shame! Rise up, shake off the devil, the lusts of the flesh and the shackles of your own making. Hate the devil, hate sin and hate your own weakness and lethargy. Quit being the heel that the serpent is always biting and instead become the heel that crushes the head of the serpent.

That's God's promise to you!

NOTES

OTHER BOOKS BY MICHAEL HOWARD

LOVE CONSTRAINED is the sequel to "Recklessly Abandoned" about missions work in war-torn Mocambique and how God used ordinary people to change the destiny of a nation through intercession

THE ONLY GOOD ONE IS A DEAD ONE is real stories of African snakes and how alike they are in character to the devil. An unusual look at breaking soul ties.

THE PRICE OF DISOBEDIENCE is a study on the price paid by a person, church or nation when they do not obey God's mandate for them.

WHAT IS YOUR DESTINY is a powerful exhortation to the Body of Christ today to line up with the Word of God and carry out His plan for your lives as individuals, as a Body and as a nation.

THE PERVERTED GOSPEL is an end-time book which reveals how the Body has taken different aspects of the Word and made them into Gospels thus perverting the ONLY GOSPEL.

TALES OF AN AFRICAN INTERCESSOR is a new look at intercession which will inspire and change your life and encourage you to be intercessors - the only thing that will see the Body through in these last days.

PROVEN ARROWS OF INTERCESSION is a handbook which lays out principles of intercession. Intercession is a discipline in relationship and has everything to do with knowing the heart of the Father.

THIS IS THAT is a booklet of stories compiled by W.E.C. from letters sent home to England from missionaries who experienced a tremendous outpouring and revival in the Congo in the early '50's.

SERMON ON THE MOUNT is a powerful book and takes a look in detail at each of the aspects of Christ's Sermon of Matthew and how they should become part of every believer's life.

FEASTING AT THE KING'S TABLE is a timely book on Holy Communion and our need to celebrate on a regular basis.

TO SAVE A NATION is another true tale about the results in Southern Sudan – a nation torn by the horrors of war and slavery.

CONTACTS

SHEKINAH MINISTRIES
P.O. Box 34685
Kansas City, MO 64116 USA
Tel (816) 734-0493
Fax (816) 734-0218
Email Shekmin@aol.com

SHEKINAH MINISTRIES
P.O. Box 186, Station "A"
Etobicoke M9C 1C0
Canada
Tel (416) 626-1543

SHEKINAH MINISTRIES
17 Wayside
Weston-super-Mare BS22 9BL
England
Tel 011-44-1934-629785
Email: JandH@wint829.fsnet.co.uk

KALIBU MINISTRIES
P.O. Box 1473
Blantyre, Malawi, Africa
011-265-633187

Email Kalibu@malawi.net

KALIBU MINISTRIES
P.O. Box 124
Escourt 3310,
South Africa
Tel 011-27-363-525399

KALIBU MINISTRIES
P.O. Box 55
Banket
Zimbabwe
011-263-67-26293
rozhoward@mango.zw

SHEKINAH MINISTRIES
Out of Africa
Päivölänrinne 1 E
FI-04220 Kerava
358 404 13 22 00
andreas@outofafrica.fi